"AGAINST THE BACKDROP of the Islamic Revolution, Roya Movafegh carries us with one unforgettable young woman and her family on a gripping journey into the unknown, opening a brilliant prismatic window on the power of faith and delivering a deeply affecting tale of memory, culture, and identity."

—Neda Armian (film producer, *Rachel Getting Married*)

"THE STORY HAS every element imaginable, and, most importantly, it's current, it's contemporary, it's relevant, and it's urgent—as nothing has changed to this day for the People With No Camel in their motherland. An important debut novel from a luminous author."

—Shidan Majidi (Broadway producer and director)

THE PEOPLE WITH NO CAMEL

BASED ON A TRUE STORY
Roya Movafegh

Full Court Press
Englewood Cliffs, New Jersey

First Edition

Copyright © 2010 by Roya Movafegh

Published in the United States of America
by The Writing Center
for Full Court Press,
601 Palisade Avenue
Englewood Cliffs, NJ 07632

ISBN 978-0-578-05545-9
Library of Congress Control No. 2010926079

Author Photo by Behrooz Shahidi

Editing and Book Design by Barry Sheinkopf for Bookshapers
(www.bookshapers.com)

Cover Design by Maximilian Jezo-Parovsky

Colophon by Liz Sedlack

THIS BOOK IS DEDICATED
to my parents
to my brother

and to those who stayed. . . .

According to the laws of Sharia in Iran, if a Muslim man is murdered, his family may be compensated according to the price of one hundred camels. If the same crime is committed against a Muslim woman, her family is entitled to the price of fifty camels.

If a Bahá'í is murdered, no camels apply.

I am of the People with No Camel.

THE PEOPLE
WITH NO CAMEL

Chapter One

I LIE IN THIS DESERT of no name and feel the night sky pulling me towards its limitless depths. Sparkling diamonds scattered over black velvet, I see some move and catch my breath. Why have I not seen this sky before? The city lights block our view they tell me.

Do you see me? Do you see where we're heading? Tell me your secrets. You know mine.

I close my eyes, yet the images of the day appear before me— a day unlike any other.

A GLIMPSE OF MY MOTHER at dawn. . . . "It's time," she had whispered. I had been waiting for this time. Time to be another person, to leave those I love. To leave Iran. Time, which manifested itself in my grandfather's tears. Smothered in his firm embrace, I could only hear his trembling voice, his failed attempt at words. Through his muddled sounds, I pieced together what he had meant to say: our special name one last time. The name he had made up and reserved for all his grandchildren. I had prepared myself for my mother's and grandmother's tears, not my grandfather's. In them, I understood that we were truly leaving, for real this time. We were leaving my grandparents, our friends, the sounds of bombs falling, of missiles firing. We were leaving behind the day I trembled from fear in the middle of the street during a bomb raid, as my father shook me to regain my senses. We were leaving behind good-byes unsaid, for we had only learned about our moment of escape the previous afternoon.

Above all, we were leaving behind the daily anxieties, wondering when the Pasdaran would raid our home or the homes in which we took refuge.

Throughout the silent taxi ride to the airport, occasionally interrupted by the gulping tears my mother was determined to hide, my mind lingered back to Papaji, my grandfather, a man of few words, ample logic, and moderate emotion. I was certain that my grandmother, Mamaji, was still crying. Her tears were not unfamiliar.

Our arrival at the airport grounds steered my thoughts away from my grandparents to the ascending airplanes. I joined my younger brother, Joubin, who was pasting his forehead to the side window. We covered the foggy glass beneath our breaths in "footprints" made by the sides of our fists and fingers.

Three years had passed since our last flight in 1978, when we had flown back from a month-long visit to Vienna, the birthplace of my brother and me. Between my parents, their years in Vienna lasted sixteen years, where they first met as students, married, and juggled their courses, their jobs, which including working at the Iranian Embassy—and a baby girl. Shortly after Joubin was born, they decided to move back to Tehran.

Like everything else, much had changed since the Islamic Revolution. My mother and I hadn't had to wait in the *Women* line at the airport back in 1978. Now, a black-veiled security guard called for me to approach. Her voice exuded authority; her eyes were devoid of warmth. She searched my body, much like one would search for valuables on a fresh corpse, and I in turn searched for a sign that would tell me that she had once been a girl like me. At the end, it seemed that neither one of us found what we sought. I waited on the sidelines until my mother, too, passed through the hurried and unkind hands of the guard.

During our flight to Zahedan, Joubin called out "Mommy" to show the results of the light-producing button by his seat.

"Tell him to call you 'Mother' instead of 'Mommy'," came our father's whisper to our mother.

"How about I call you *Nanneh?*" said Joubin, leading to laughter we all needed.

I looked at him as he continued his fascination with the light button. He doesn't understand what's happening, I thought. He doesn't know that soon his name will change. He's five. He thinks we're going to build sand castles near our grandparents' villa in *Shomal*. Mom and Dad can't tell him that we're escaping to Pakistan. He may tell if questioned by authorities, and all would be over. I understand. I'm ten, and I understand.

I *did* understand—the basics. Life in Iran had become unrecognizable to most of us, though a welcomed change to those who had suffered under the Shah's rule, mainly those with few means.

Not a single day had passed since the Revolution without an array of small printed faces covering the pages of newspapers, faces that had met the firing squads or the knotted ropes of those who had betrayed the Islamic Republic. Their crimes ranged from previous associations with the Shah's regime to speaking or acting out against the new Islamic government. The Pasdaran would find their "obstructers" of the Islamic Republic mostly through home raids.

News articles, without faces, told of lashes granted to those who sullied "Islamic laws" in other ways, like playing music or cards, owning alcohol, or appearing in inappropriate dress—like the story of the father and daughter who had been arrested after swimming in their garden pool. They had received lashes for wearing bathing suits, for exposing skin to one another. The fifteen-year-old daughter had fainted after receiving a number of lashes, and the father had begged to receive her remaining counts in addition to his own.

Life in Iran as Bahá'ís changed, too. The thirteen-decade promises of our extinction were suddenly amplified under the Islamic Regime. Our executions were reported in the state-owned newspapers, but not our stories—those were shared personally among households. I'm glad we live in Tehran, I often thought as I sipped my *chaee* while listening to what was befalling our relatives and friends. At least here, our homes aren't burned as much as in the smaller cities or villages. We knew of many who had become homeless, dispersed among family and friends who had space for this child or that grandmother.

At least Mr. Saraj had some warning. There had been a rumor. His Muslim niece begged him to store his valuables at her home. He brought one box—the only piece not destroyed by the fire that consumed everything his family had owned. When he opened that box, his niece sobbed uncontrollably. The box was filled with Bahá'í books.

Every day, everywhere, faces, numbers, and rumors streamed through living rooms, the corner stores, the cab drivers.

I thought nothing of my endless drawings of men tied to posts, crying as bullets exploded out of firing squad rifles. During one of my great-uncle's visit to my grandparents, I had proudly shown one of those drawings to him, awaiting praise and recognition for my skills and choice of colors.

"Look at what our children are drawing," he said, his distaste undeniable.

I looked. What was wrong with what I'd drawn? I looked. Then I saw. Then wished that I hadn't drawn it.

I GRAB A HANDFUL OF pebbles and dust from the desert. My fists clench tightly over the coarse edges, pressing them deep into my skin, waiting for the pain to convince me that I'm not in a dream. It does, and I let the rocks fall back to the ground through my fingers. Now, I dream about the fish and the rice we ate in Zahedan. Had I known that we would now be eating stale bread and cheese, I would have chewed slower. I would have held the fork of rice under my nose longer, allowing the scent of saffron to linger.

But my attention had not been on the meal then. My thoughts had been with my father, wondering how he knew the two men he had greeted upon our entry into the motel lobby in Zahedan; wondering why they were all pretending not to know each other ten minutes later in the motel restaurant, even as they sat at nearby tables; wondering where my dad was heading as he rose from his seat mid-meal; wondering whether the man with the black hair and mustache he had greeted earlier was also heading the same way; wondering why we suddenly had to rush through sipping our *doogh* after my father returned to our table; wondering about that and more.

Now I know that they had been friends all along—that one of those men, Hamid, a slim man in his late twenties who looked like he wouldn't find many things funny, had followed my father out of the restaurant to give him the key to our room. In that room, I received answers to some of my questions. Joubin and I had climbed onto the bed and lay there motionless, staring at the ceiling cracks, while our parents quickly unpacked our Baluch clothes to be worn for our disguise. I took off my navy corduroy pants to wear the loose and baggy pants and the matching top that came down to my knees. I liked the little red-and-white flowered patterns. I had seen my mother sewing our cotton clothes the week before.

"These pants are too big," Joubin said, looking down at his beige outfit.

"They're not big. That's the style. They're called *shalvar khamis*. You'll see how comfortable they are," my mother said, hastily dressing him.

Minutes later, our parents packed the clothes we had changed out of and we were ready to leave, but not before we learned and practiced our new names.

"Mansur Khan"— a weighty name to carry for a five-year-old, I thought. It is not an uncommon name among the Baluch, my father told us, and neither is our mother's name. Her name would stay "Khandan". He was to be known as "Mohammad Shah Nasser". His name made sense, befitting a grown man.

My new name was Golbakht—"Flowered Fortune". I became a Baluch girl from Afghanistan.

IN THAT ROOM, WE left behind a life that had been and emerged as villagers.

Led by my father, we disappeared through the back motel door to avoid attracting attention. During our stroll down the road, he dropped our three little bags into a parked pick-up truck as we continued to walk.

Questions were piling up in my mind. Why had we discarded our last remnants from home, packed down to three small hand-bags? Why were the two men from the motel crossing the street and heading directly towards us? Why did they walk with my father? Why were there no greetings or words? Had we run into them by chance, or had it been planned? Did my father know them? How did he know them? How long would we wander about in the streets together?

I wanted to return to the room. I knew that my questions couldn't be asked then, for the streets had ears.

Walk about aimlessly—we'll find you! were Hamid's instructions from the smugglers, I learned later, and so we roamed, men in front, children and woman steps behind.

As we walked, I became engrossed by the moving images of life within Zahedan: Baluch boys selling Fanta by the roadside, old men with yellow-white beards sitting among their overstocked goods of colanders, baskets, and toys hanging from every inch of space.

"Smaller streets!" we heard a man's voice say from a passing white pick-up truck.

Led by Hamid, we entered dirt roads that contained few shops with no windows, no doors, merely rugs that hung from the walls and ceilings, making the otherwise barren road come alive.

"Quick, get in!" said Hamid's friend Nasser, who was a slightly thinner man with hazel hair and most likely in his late twenties as well.

A truck pulled up from behind. That's when I first discovered the deception of time. My body moved quickly to get into the truck, yet part of me remained on the sidewalk, still and unaffected by motion.

Joubin and I were silent as we sped down side roads, vaguely hearing the murmurs of our father and Hamid. The roads and the people they carried intrigued me: an old man walking by his donkey; a mother balancing a large plastic container on her head, dragging a small child beside her; two old men squatting by the road drinking *chaee*; three boys running after another boy on a bicycle. I watched, envious of their unhurried walks, routine errands, and play.

A group of kids ran alongside our truck, screaming and laughing, until we stopped in the middle of their little village. We stared at one another and exchanged only silence. As we hurried from the van to the little hut, I took in as much as I could, the roaming goats, the little boy who followed the smallest of the goats, his need for new shoes.

Inside the hut, we were greeted by a village man who wore gray Baluch clothes, with an added white cloth draped around his head and over his shoulder. He couldn't have been more than forty, yet his thin face bore deep creases, like those of the rest of the men in his village. Would a palm reader have been able to read those lines, too? If not, his deep dark eyes would surely speak. It knew things, different from what we knew.

The village man introduced us to a woman sitting nearby with her two children, wearing clothes similar to ours. They, like Hamid and Nasser, also didn't bear the faces or hands of villagers, hands that showed the calluses of daily chores, as did the dirt under their fingernails.

The little boy, who seemed a year older than Joubin, leaned against his sister, who was not a child, not a woman. Murmurs of the plans continued as my mind wandered to the interior walls and floors of the hut, which were overwhelmed by myriads of coinciding colors. We sat on layers of Persian rugs that covered the ground. A veiled woman served us *chaee* with *ghand*. Life took place near the ground, with little use for furniture. The sound of the boiling water was soothing. It was a sound I knew. It took me back to some of my favorite living rooms back home, in the company of loved ones, eating dried mulberries with tea, overhearing discussions about the high prices for salt, the two-day queues for gas, and the increased abductions of Bahá'ís.

A glance at the woman sitting with her two kids hauled me back to the village hut. She too sat silently observing, occasionally biting her lower lip.

"We're about to leave for the border," my father whispered to us before we rose to leave the hut. A young rooster hurried away as we stepped outside.

"Where's your *chador*?" the village man asked my mother.

"I just have this shawl," she responded, looking as if she had just realized that she'd forgotten her house keys at home.

A village woman who was feeding a group of chickens nearby lost her chador with one pull from the village man.

"You still don't look like one of us. Wear this," he said, and disappeared without another word.

"Thank you," mumbled my mother to his shadow, and held up the veil. Old and dusty, its musty odor wafted about, reaching me standing a foot away. I watched her staring at the veil for a while longer before she pulled it over her head.

Villagers don't call their moms *Mommy,* I reminded myself.

The continued murmurs between Hamid and the village man were drowned by the blaring noises of two motorcyclists. Mesmerized, Joubin and I watched as they sped by, leaving behind a trail of racing children, screaming in play.

"They're ready," said Nasser, nodding to my father, as he headed towards a dusty red pick-up truck that awaited our ascent. My mother took Joubin's hand in hers, climbed into the front seat, and pulled him up on her lap. The other mother, as she sat next to mine, did the same with her son. My father called my name, then helped me climb onto the rear load of the truck. I noticed something familiar leaning against the corner: our three little handbags. Home.

It was part of the murmur plans all along, I said to myself. I wanted to call out to my brother, but I knew it had to wait. Time moved fast, and tensions lay heavy.

I drifted somewhere between keeping up with the piling of the rest of us unto the truck and dreaming about when I would tell Joubin that our bags had been found—that he hadn't lost his cowboy gun and his favorite blue Hot Wheels with white stripes. Nor had I lost my yellow Snow White and Seven Dwarfs wallet, or my miniature green container on a string that held three tiny dice—our only treasures from home, small and light, two items each, as our parents had instructed.

My father placed a blanket beneath me and told me to lean against our bags. Traces of home cushioned me from the hard surface of the truck. The other daughter sat close against her bundles. A kneeling Hamid turned to us girls. "Whenever we stop, you must pretend to be asleep," he said, with his piercing black eyes. His voice, though calm, made it clear that it was not to be crossed. "Whenever, wherever! You must pretend to be sleeping. Do you understand?"

We understood, and we nodded. He removed his long stare from us when the village man's holler set us in motion. The same children whose excited cries had carried us into their village reappeared and ran alongside us again in the dusty roads. I watched; they ran, shouted, and waved.

The motorcyclists led the way in wavy motions. We could hear them even when we could no longer see them. Within minutes of our drive, I began feeling grateful for the canvas sheets beneath us, as well as the bags against us. Every passing pot hole lifted our bodies and thumped them back down. My father's exaggerated cries made us both laugh; the laughter became contagious, at least to the other daughter. In the midst of receiving our bruises, she introduced herself as Layla. Not much more could be heard, for the engine was loud and our bodies lurching.

The two motorcyclists disappeared and reappeared sporadically, lingering for a second, before setting out in opposite directions.

"Why do they do this?" I asked my father.

"They're our eyes in front and behind us," he replied.

My senses were overtaken by the sounds of the engine, the tires passing through dust, the bashing of our bodies, and the laughter of my father and me. Layla was no longer laughing. After a particularly painful bump, he said, "Good to have many ribs. One or two broken won't be such a loss." We laughed again, though that mood changed quickly at the border.

Our truck slowed down, and Hamid's stern eyes reminded me of what I needed to do. Layla and I shut our eyes, but my mind wandered to my brother in the front seat. He too must be *sleeping,* I thought. We had stopped. Voices escalated. My curiosity took hold, and I felt compelled to peek through my eyelids as a male voice moved closer to the rear of our truck. I had great trust in my method of peeking, for I had used it on my parents on countless occasions without fail. Only able to see shapes and shadows,

I did not dare open my lids further. A guard in army clothes stood before us, machine gun in hand. I then understood why Hamid had ordered us to sleep, for I was certain that my eyes would have betrayed us all. I closed my eyes completely and only relied on sounds. The village man's voice was distressed.

"Our chief is sick. It'll bring us shame if we don't visit him!" he shouted.

The voice of the guard overpowered his, a voice cold with contempt. "I said go back! Will not say it again! I'll shoot you all if you don't turn back right now!"

I prayed that the guard could not hear the pounding heart underneath my frozen shell. I didn't hear any other words, just the sound of our engine. We reversed and drove away. I opened my eyes and saw Hamid and Nasser engrossed in murmurs. My father's gaze was fixed upon the murmurs, but his expression was unfamiliar. I had no intention or desire to ask or say anything. My heart was still racing. We were surrounded by dry desert, gray hills, and more gray mountains. My body ached from all the bruising from the unforgiving roads. I could no longer find any humor in it. It seemed that my father couldn't either. He hadn't made a sound since we had left the guards. We passed another deep pot hole, and our bodies crashed against the truck. The pain surpassed that of the other times, but I wasn't going to cry.

Suddenly, we heard emerging sounds of helicopters, though we couldn't see them. I began to pray in panic. I had heard stories about these helicopters, looking for anyone attempting to escape. I knew that, if we were detected, we'd be arrested, and prison meant torture. I fought with the images of a hot iron passing over my father's body, like the Pasdaran had done to our Bahá'í friend in Hamadan.

The sounds faded and eventually disappeared. We continued on, but not for much longer. Our truck slowed down and came to a halt. Hamid and Nasser seemed anxious. The village man stepped out of the truck, and Hamid and Nasser joined him. All I could hear were murmurs. I was asleep.

"You can open your eyes," said my father to me. "No one's around. Did well."

His attention drifted back to Hamid and Nasser; mine traveled back to the guard with the icy voice.

"The last pot hole damaged the transmission," said Hamid, motioning towards my father. "The driver's going to have to go back to try to fix it. We'll have to wait until he returns."

My father was silent.

Here? I wanted to shout, but only followed my father's silent composure. The desert stretched far and wide. We began our descent from the truck, gathering some canvas sheets. We watched as the village man climbed the truck and drove away with the motorcyclists.

The hills as our refuge, we sat, and we waited. I was happy to be sitting with my mother and brother again. I didn't want to ask them what they had seen from the front seat of the truck. I didn't want to speak about the guard, and it seemed they didn't either.

The other mother offered us some bread, cheese, and water she had been carrying in one of her bags. Joubin and I ate very little, preferring to find pebbles to throw down the hill, watching them tumble below. Our mother sat nearby, her veil resting on her shoulders. Few words passed among her, Layla, and her mother. Layla's brother wasn't interested in throwing stones. "I want to go home," he complained in a refrain that quickly culminated in tears and wailing. He seemed more lost than any of us in that land empty of anything familiar. We bore his discontentment, mostly because we didn't have a choice, or maybe because he was acting out what must have lain within us all.

The distant sound of a helicopter shifted us all into agitation. Hamid screamed, "Canvas!" and everyone ran towards the sheets. My mother reached for hers, quickly made us lie on the ground, and fully covered us. "Don't move!" she commanded. We didn't. Not a muscle. The escalating sounds of helicopters that crept near made me wish that we were hiding in one of those burrows I had seen in the war movies, in which the Yugoslav soldiers hid the village kids beneath the ground to protect them from the German Army. Black and white World War II films, on repeat, had been our only source of entertainment during the war with Iraq.

I didn't know where my father was. He had been speaking to Hamid when we first heard the helicopter, and I hoped that he was well hidden. Though my heart was pounding, I was happy that Joubin was near me. This was not the first time we had huddled together, taking refuge. We were familiar with huddling underneath something, like the dining table, together with our playmates, during a bomb raid. We spent hours playing under that table with pillows and cushions, dolls and cars, food and water. And now we lay in the open desert and wished we were under a table.

Like the other times, the sounds from the sky subsided and we emerged from our hiding spots.

"Didn't you have enough canvas to cover yourself?" asked the other mother when she saw our mother's veil covering her body like a blanket.

"It wasn't big enough for the three of us, but the colors of this veil blend in with these hills," she replied with a half smile.

My eyes searched for my father, and I was relieved to see him climbing toward us.

The other mother offered us more bread. We ate it, and waited in the desert for hours.

THE HILLS AND ROADS are blending into one another. I scoop another handful of tiny rocks. Slowly, I release them from the side of my fist onto the floral patterns on my pants, covering my entire thighs with dry earth. I look at my dusty hands. They look like Golbakht's.

Along with the last remaining rays of the sun crept fear.

"What if he's not coming back?" I heard Layla say, mostly to herself, as we all sat together in wait on the arid grounds.

Her words suddenly took me to a black-and-white photograph I had seen at the home of family friends, taken in 1979, of some of the two thousand Bahá'ís who had been exiled from their small village in Boyr-e Ahmad. They were farmers, carpet weavers, charcoal producers, leather makers. They were women, men, children—exiled to the desert, with only a minimum of their livestock to keep them from starving. The image showed eight rows of people posing for the camera, the first three of which were children, squatting on the desert ground. Only one person stood apart, a few feet away in the front: a little child no more than three or four, who seemed to look straight into my eyes from the photograph. Whether that child was a boy or a girl, I couldn't tell even by looking at his or her short unkempt hair, loose baggy pants, or tight top.

After many letters and pleadings from the Bahá'í communities to the Islamic Republic, the four hundred and fifty families were finally allowed to return to their village, in addition to the two infants that had been born during their forty-five days of exile. One, a baby girl, was named Tahirih after the great scholar and poetess who was the first woman to lift her veil in Iran in 1848, to demonstrate a break from Islamic law after she became a follower of the Báb. The other, a baby boy, was called Badi in memory of a seventeen-year-old Bahá'í youth tortured and killed in 1869 for carrying a tablet written by Bahá'u'lláh to Nasiri'd-Din Shah Qajar.

"He'll be here," Nasser said calmly, not looking away from his thoughts as he stroked his mustache.

"But they're drug smugglers, after all," Layla's mother said suddenly. "How do you know you can trust them?"

"Cause I *know!*" Nasser said dryly, turning to her. "He'll be here." There wasn't a trace of doubt in his voice or thin face, so I decided to believe him.

Everyone prepared their resting spot before all daylight was lost.

At dawn, we had left our grandparents; at dusk, my brother and I lay next to our parents and faced the sky in that nameless desert. "It's so dark," I whispered to my father.. "How will they know where to find us out here?"

"They'll find us," he said calmly. "They know these hills like the backs of their hands, feeling their way through. They don't need to see."

I held my hands up to the stars and only saw shadows. Slowly, I directed my right middle finger over to the back of my left hand, around and between every bone, knuckle, and web.

"Remember the heat of the day," said my father. "It'll help keep you warm." We lay and remembered and at times were comforted but mostly struggled to remember harder.

Nestled together for warmth, my mind wandered forward, trying to picture the next Pakistani border, but mostly found myself drifting back to my friends at home. Were they seeing the moon that very moment? Were they seeing it from their beds? I longed to be with them. I longed to be in my bed.

I HAD NOT SEEN MY friends for weeks. My parents had pulled my brother and me out of school for fear that the Pasdaran would come for us. My mother taught my lessons at home, a welcome idea at first: no more lengthy walks in the early hours of the morning, no more shared commutes in crowded taxis, staring at the weary expressions worn by so many. Few passengers dared to speak out against the Islamic Republic during these rides, though every so often one would, releasing what many held in. Then we'd hope that those comments wouldn't fall in the laps of those who supported the regime. The shortage of gas had lumped us all together, strangers from all walks of life, sharing rides with whoever would pass—taxis, vans, and trucks of every shape and size. At times it was thrilling. I felt lucky to be riding in a semi with my father, high off the ground, passing life below.

Yet as luck goes, it lands both ways. Other times, it lands next to a driver in a pick-up truck, one who is discreet, whom I had to sit beside, along with my brother and mother, and who rested his two fingers on my upper thighs.

I had felt the violent beating of my heart in my head. Why was he doing that? I'd peeked at my mother, who was looking ahead at the road. I had wanted to scream out to her but instead used the German books from my lap to push away his fingers, only to have him reposition them slyly against my bottom. I'd wanted to hit him with my books, to throw us out of his truck. Instead, numb and mute, I had pleaded for it to end.

"What's the matter?" my mother had asked me upon our descent. I'd told her.

"Why didn't you *say* something?" she had cried, bewildered. "And I even paid him!" There we'd stood by the side of the road, hearing only the sound of the flowing waters of the *joob*, smelling the heat and my mother's rage. My brother and I had both watched her in silence.

"I was scared he was going to hurt us," I'd mumbled finally.

"I would have hurt *him*!" she had exclaimed, then drawn me in and held me close. We had continued on our way, each alone with our thoughts.

Less commuting meant less gambling with luck. I was happy to stay home, yet what I hadn't foreseen was how deeply I would miss my friends, the remaining ones. I had been through much with them. The years we had spent together at the German School of Tehran had been carefree, but then had come the Revolution, and with it the overturning of a life we had once recognized.

Each change forced us to adapt, at least on the surface—from the closing of our foreign schools, to holding classes at a schoolmate's house; from spending half our lifetimes together, to seeing the Germans among us leave our country and our lives.

Those of us who had remained returned to the grounds of our old German school, only it'd no longer felt like a place we knew. Even then, we were happy not to be dispersed further. Our command of Farsi didn't equate to the Iranian schools' standards; hence we were placed in a special classroom.

Two years earlier, we had rallied together, shouting protests after the rumored departure of our second-grade teacher; two years later, we had gasped when one of us was slapped by our new teacher for giggling nervously while struggling to answer a question.

The changes had come faster than we could assimilate them— exchanging our rejuvenating swimming lessons for lessons in tying headscarves and wearing long-sleeved uniforms; finding our field trips to farms and mountains mutate into roles in plays depicting scenes of the Iran-Iraq war, dying as martyrs; moving from school-age love triangles to watching stubbly masons build walls dividing our school grounds into girls' and boys' sections. The boys had laughed at first, until the bricks reached our eye level.

A year and a half later, I too had left my friends. These were the friends that had never turned their backs on me, never called me *nadjes*—a privilege, I thought, thinking back to my friend Sahar, when she was still living in Zahedan and was expelled from several schools for denying that she was dirty.

My mother's attempt at home schooling had lasted three weeks before my father surprised us by coming home early one afternoon.

She'd gasped, "Why are you. . .what's happened?"

"Hello!" he said brightly as Joubin climbed onto his shoulders.

"It's so early," she had said.

"Wanted to have tea at home," he'd replied in the midst of balancing my wrestling brother on his shoulder and simultaneously hugging me.

My parents stood in the foyer with their *chaees* at hand, and my father recounted what had taken place earlier that morning. His new executive director at the Carpet Manufacturing Company, Mr. Kazemi, had called him to his office. "He told me that he has a promotion in mind for me at the Ministry of Commerce."

"But that's great!" my mother'd said quickly.

"No, no, wait! Mr. Kazemi said, 'But, we need people we can trust. Who are in line with *our* ideas.' So I told him that, judging from the anti-Bahá'í book that he had left on my desk, I was assuming that he was referring to my Faith."

"And then?" My mother's eyes had grown wide.

"That's when he said,'You don't have to make this complicated, Mr. Movafegh. Just recant. Your career depends on it.' And I told him, 'You speak of trust, yet you ask me to deny my Faith for a position. If I was capable of that, wouldn't I just as easily be capable of denying you for a better deal in the future?'"

"What did he say?" she'd asked when he paused to sip his tea.

"He said, 'Very well! That leaves us no choice but to go before the board.' He called the meeting, and we met with them. He told them that I couldn't continue my position there, and the chairman quickly interrupted and asked, 'Why?' I turned to Mr. Kazemi and said, 'Do you want to tell them, or should I?' He didn't say anything, so I told them that I was being fired because I'm a Bahá'í. The chairman said, 'So you're a Bahá'í—and. . . ?' Then Kazemi raised his voice and said, 'He's "of them"'!"

My father shook his head and continued calmly, "The chairman became very angry and shouted, 'This *Bahá'í* director saw us through the toughest times of this company. He took care of us!' But all Kazemi said was, 'I have my instructions! We can't work with people that are "of them." The Ministry will decide this matter,' and he stormed out of the meeting. A half hour later, I was called back to Kazemi's office. He told me that I had caused uproar in the company. He said I had one last chance, 'One day, to publicly repudiate this so-called Faith of yours. Recant or lose your position.' I immediately told him that I didn't need a day to refuse his offer."

She had stared blankly at him and asked, "Now what?" her face pale, her voice broken.

"Now, we'll have more tea, and in two days I'm to go back to the office to receive my compensation."

Two days later, my father had returned home, only this time he had been pale in the face.

"Kazemi wants me to pay *them* back," he'd said.

"Pay what back?" she'd asked.

"Three years of salary," he had said, as if he was answering my mother while listening to something else, only there wasn't any-thing else to hear. Whatever my mother was trying to say in re-sponse had not culminated in words, though they seemed to be perched on the tip of her tongue. I kept eyeing the clear glass of *chaee* she had in her hand, which was gradually tilting, the auburn edging closer to the rim. I'd wanted to warn her but felt it best to stay silent until it became truly necessary to save the carpet, not because I cared much about the carpet, but it would be one less thing to become upset about.

"I asked him how long I had to pay the sum," my father had continued. "He said a week!"

My mother had finally mustered her words. "I don't under-stand."

"He said that, as a Bahá'í, actually to quote him exactly, '*as one of you*, you shouldn't have been eligible to receive a salary.'"

As he turned to leave the room, my mother's mouth had moved, yet for a while no sound had come. "Where're you going?"

"We can't wait any longer. It needs to happen now. I'll be late," he said and left the house.

The next three days spun our parents out of our reach, our home schooling replaced by our mother's ceaseless sewing, and our father a mere shadow in the late and early hours of the day. My grandparents would arrive by noon, with hot meals in hand, and spend the afternoons with Joubin and me, which meant that Papaji would be tied to a chair with jump rope and padlocks, a practice my brother had taken up and skillfully mastered, and which was patiently tolerated by our grandfather.

"Okay, Papaji, now free yourself," my brother would say boastfully. And at times our grandfather would untangle himself successfully, giggling all the while.

By late afternoon, we would gather our things, drive back to my grandparents', and spend the night with them. My father hadn't wanted to increase the chances of night raids, which were by then more of a threat than ever. This was the case not only because of the rise in raids of Bahá'í homes. We were still mourning the loss of our National Bahá'í governing council, whose nine members had been abducted from their houses and disappeared without a trace. But my father's fears were also rooted in Kazemi's last words to him when he had threatened a call to the Pasdaran if the Board stood up for my father again and caused further disturbances.

In between bouts of my mother's incessant sewing, we managed a visit to one of her close friends, Nooshin, whose home I had often frequented to receive my one-on-one art lessons with her husband, Behrooz. That day, Nooshin sat in her long green '70s robe and knitted me a little brown pouch.

"Here, my dear. You can wear this around your neck during the next little while and remember that we all love you very much."

Those three days had set in motion the five turbulent days of going into hiding in preparation for our escape.

Our first hiding spot had been at the home of one of my father's colleagues. Like us, they also lived in one of the outskirts of Tehran. His wife, Shiva, was pregnant, beautiful, and a lover of Barbara Streisand. We prepared meals together, ate together, and listened to *Woman In Love* more than seven times a day. Her passion for her song grew on me, and I found myself humming the melody during our breaks from listening to the LP. Everything in their home had taken on Streisand's voice for me—their dark brown leather couches, their glass tables, and the white wall-to-wall carpets throughout the two-story edifice.

My father and his colleague were only home in the evenings. My mother's nights were spent pacing in their living room until dawn—and her days reflected her nights, her face no longer bearing her name, Khandan, which means 'in a state of laughter,' though it had been a befitting name up to a couple of months before we went into hiding.

Joubin passed many hours on the ground playing with his blue-and-white Hot Wheels. I occupied myself by looking through their record collection, as I often did with my older cousin, Schabi, at our grandparent's giant and ancient gramophone, playing my aunt's collection of Nana Mouskouri and Jacques Brel.

One afternoon, Shiva and I sat on the carpet in the room that was to be their baby's, which only held a white crib and our family's bedding.

"Are you having a boy or a girl?" I asked her.

"I don't know," she answered, holding her roundness. "What do you think?"

I shrugged. "Will this room stay like this?"

"I'm going to put up a few pictures. And a rocking chair," she added, and I could almost see the envisioned room in her eyes. I didn't know how long we were to stay in hiding with them before our moment of escape, but I wished it to be long enough for me to see their baby.

On the fourth night, we moved locations and slept at the home of long-time family friends. Even I knew that they were risking much to give us refuge. That night, well past my bedtime, I could still overhear the voices of my mother and Khaleh Farideh, the longest I had heard my mother talking in a long time. The next night, we returned to my grandparents for our final evening in Tehran.

Not until years later did I learn that my father hadn't told my mother that we were to leave Iran the following morning. He had kept this information from her in part due to her already evident anguish, but also as a result of the insistence of her parents that he escape Iran first and send for us after. Their logic was rooted in the fact that my mother was not a Bahá'í at the time, and that therefore she and their grandchildren would be safe with them— an opinion my mother was leaning towards. Yet my father had no intention of leaving Joubin and me behind. In my grandparents' fears, they hadn't foreseen that their daughter would have been considered as *nadjes* as her husband and her children, for marriage to a Bahá'í became an act against the Islamic Republic as well.

FAINT SOUNDS STIRRED US into silence in the dark desert. With canvases at hand, everyone turned to Hamid for direction. Though nothing could be seen but the stars, we hid beneath our canvases, waiting to determine whether those sounds of motors were what we had awaited or feared.

Out of darkness emerged four headlights, headed for us. Were the lights those of the village man or the Pasdaran prowling around for their prey?

The lights and the sounds stopped. And for a moment so did

our lungs, until we heard Hamid cry, "Let's go!"

With great relief and disbelief, we gathered our things and headed towards the truck and the motorcycles.

I gladly bore the bumps of the ride, as we were in motion again, fast on our way to somewhere—away from the exposed vastness. Unwavering and without headlights, our pickup truck plowed through turns and up steep hills in complete dark.

Not long after, we reached a small village where men spoke in a tongue that sounded almost familiar. We followed the village man into a small hut, similar to the one we had stopped in earlier that day. In this one, however, men and women sat separately. A veiled woman brought us *chaee*. Warmth entered our bodies, and I hoped that we wouldn't have to leave that hut for some time. I paid little attention to the heavy murmurs among the men. My brother, and the other little boy, cuddled up to their mothers and took comfort in sipping their *chaees*. A little girl crawled away from the village woman's lap. Her feet were bare, her hair unkempt, her clothes dusty, her face sweet.

Suddenly, my attention was drawn to the far side of the room, the men's side, as the village man tore a paper bill in half. Why does he destroy money—money that could be used for new shoes? Why does he give the torn half to Hamid and return the other to his own pocket?

I searched for clues in my parents' faces but saw only silence, a silence I knew was not to be broken. The men's murmurs continued. I drew close to my mother.

"Will we stay here tonight?" I whispered.

"No, just waiting for the right moment to leave," she whispered back.

"When?"

"We're waiting for the guard at the border to go on his tea break. We'll go when he leaves."

My heart started jumping every which way. Maybe we should head back home, I wanted to suggest, a second before realizing that we didn't have a home anymore. Maybe we could go back to living with Shiva. But what if word got out that we were hiding in their neighborhood? It wasn't only the Pasdaran who took the words of the Islamic clergy to heart, words that turned us into what we ourselves didn't recognize. *How can we let these infidels sully Islam like this?* the Imams would ask during their sermons. *Do you know what these spies of Israel do in their so-called "meetings"? Their kids are all bastard children.*

And among some, the killing of a Bahá'í was seen as a good deed, much like the behavior of the mob that had attacked Sahar's father, who had been a prisoner of Zahedan for years, tortured, and eventually released only to be welcomed by the severed head of his Bahá'í friend at his doorstep. Shortly after, his family had moved to Tehran and been forced to be scattered between the homes of different relatives. When news traveled that he was a Bahá'í, he and several others were severely burned at his factory by townsmen. Dental records revealed his identity, calling his family to him, as well as the Pasdaran who had been looking for him. Their uncle tried to protect his young girls by telling them that the bandaged and blood-covered body before them, scarcely bearing life, was a friend of their father's. But they knew that they were seeing their own father. The youngest daughter vomited, while the Pasdaran waited in the hallway to arrest him in case he survived.

"He needs a new cornea?" his wife had asked the doctor.

"A *Bahá'í* cornea," the doctor emphasized.

"Corneas have religions?"

"A Muslim cornea cannot be transplanted into a Bahá'í body."

A short time later, her husband lost his vision in one eye, and he was pronounced dead not long after. But he wasn't gone, much to his brother's disbelief, when he came to claim his body at the morgue. The morsel of life that still remained in him, his brother managed to save by sneaking him out of the hospital and out of the country with his wife and three young children.

How did they know when he would take his tea break? How did they know how long he would be away from his post?

In the midst of my silent questions, Joubin complained of not feeling well. My mother held his forehead, then her own, and with reassuring words laid his head on her lap.

"How do you feel?" she asked me moments later.

I felt lightheaded and said so. Moving her gaze in my father's direction, she waited for him to turn his face towards us. Though he was only sitting three meters away, it seemed like an ocean. When his eyes met hers, she pointed to her head, then to Joubin's, and twirled her finger in the air. My father's whisper to Hamid was followed by a nod to us and a silent indication that it would pass.

Our travel companion, the other mother, held her careworn face in her palm. Her son lay asleep in her lap, his body resting on the worn-out layers of Persian rugs. I envied his moment of oblivion, and I craved sleep, yet all I could do was to join in on the anxious wait for the guard's tea break.

When that moment finally came, I rose to follow everyone into the cold night air, leaving part of me behind, fixed to the ground in that little hut.

Again, mothers and sons sat in the front, this time next to our new driver. The rest of us dispersed among the covered loads of the who-knows-what our truck was carrying. I was just relieved that I was positioned next to my father. A man from this new village ascended the truck with us and sat against the rear corner with his rifle, which at once made me feel both safe and unsafe. Were they expecting to shoot the guard, in case we ran into him?

Hamid climbed onto the truck, repeating the villager's departing words, words that must have been offered for God's protection, for *Khoda* was the only word that I understood.

Buried beneath layers of blankets and canvas, I reached for my father's firm and cushiony hand. I had always loved holding it yet never felt so intent on not letting go.

"I'm still dizzy," I told him.

"It was the tea. We weren't used to it," he reassured me.

He explained in a calm voice that the border was not far, and that it would all turn out all right. I felt slightly more comforted when he mentioned that Pari joon, his mother, who had been living in America, had been praying for us. I replayed my grandmother's chanting prayers in my ears. The force of her melodious voice had always made me find the home inside me.

We drove out of the village at the same speed that had brought us there. Before long, our truck slowed down enough to pass over uneven terrain, leading to heavier blows against the steel bed beneath us.

My father's bare whisper made its way to me beneath the blankets: "We're entering the river to cross the border. It's safer. We need to be completely quiet."

We inched forth in the shallow waters—no engine, no sound, no headlights. I was sure that my father could sense the wild pulse beating through my body.

I imagined the invisible line that lay ahead. I had become aware of the power of such lines in those World War II movies.

Our pace slowed down even further, and I knew then that we were passing the border. Cradling my hand tighter in my father's, I held on to my grandmother's prayers and took in every sound, every movement.

An eternity passed before our truck stopped, started its engine, and increased speed. The rise onto patchy ground marked our emergence from the river. During the acceleration over the hills, Hamid pulled the blankets away from our heads.

"We passed the border. We're in *Pakistan!*" he shouted.

Air moved through our lungs again.

"Ha-hah!" shouted my father, a cry reserved only for the best goals in soccer, though no goal had ever warranted the zeal we heard that night.

Though Hamid's face was hidden in the darkness, I knew that he was wearing at least a half smile. I had heard it in his voice.

I laughed along with my father, relieved and free as we continued to lie in our tight spaces facing the sky. We marveled at two shooting stars, one chasing the other.

"Do you know what they're telling you?" he asked me.

"No," I said, awaiting his reply.

"They're telling you that you're free."

His words brought rushing back our days in hiding, the months of living through bomb scares, the long queues for food and gas in the middle of winter, the constant fear of arrest and tor- ture—all of which now lay behind the border, a mile away. With nothing but sky above, I felt light, a free person entering a new land.

My mind played scenes I envisioned of Pakistan. Were we heading to a hotel like the one in Dizin? Would we snuggle by the fireplace and drink hot cocoa, then go skiing the next day? Would we call Pari joon to tell her that her prayers had just been an- swered? And suddenly I was pulled back to that night in my bed- room, as I had looked up at the moon from my bed after my prayers and had thought about Pari joon living in America. I had known that she had been praying for us for years. That knowledge had become a source of comfort for me, a way of feeling her pres- ence, her strong spirit. Yet that night in my bed, it had felt differ- ent. It had struck me that, though my grandmother ached for our safety and protection, she was living free overseas and could never know life as we lived it. Despite her distress, she could never truly know our fears, feel our weariness, or see the way we looked for justice in the every day, for her freedom veiled her from the pulse of our existence.

Now we were lying in the back of a truck in the desert—now we were free. Only now, we were on the other side and could no longer know what awaited those we had left back home. Now, I was my grandmother praying for those *I* had left behind.

My mind depleted, my body exhausted, I hid my emotions deep within, safely out of view, neatly out of touch.

I mustn't miss a shooting star. I had counted sixteen thus far.

"Where do the stars disappear to when they shoot across the sky?" I asked my father.

I was basking in his full attention. The day had brought streams of questions, the most burning ones at the tip of my tongue. Why had the village man torn his money? Why had he given Hamid a *half money*?

I could at last receive my answers.

"The half money is our protector. The village man will wait for our driver to return his missing piece, once he's taken us to a town."

What my father didn't tell me then was that the half money was not only our protector, but the driver's as well. For the missing piece was what would allow him to keep his payment and his life.

My father and I spoke for what seemed like hours under the boundless sky. Thoughts turned into words, and words drifted into sleep.

I briefly awakened as my father attempted to lift me from our tight space.

"We're there?" I mumbled.

"Not yet. We need to wait here for a while."

I could see only shadows, as we descended to the ground. I felt my mother's arms around me and was happy to feel her again. I couldn't see my brother.

"He's sleeping by the bags," she assured me as we turned to-wards him.

The cold night air was unwelcome.

"Where are we?" I asked her.

"It's a dry riverbed," she said.

I had wanted to ask how a river could run dry, but my eyes were heavy with sleep and I surrendered to it. Voices pulled me back for a moment, hearing an exchange of heated words between Hamid and the driver. Exhausted, I drifted back to sleep and was unaware of my father's departure with Hamid and the driver, as well as their arrival with a new truck. I was benumbed to the bumps, unconscious of our arrival in a new village, and dead to the remainder of the night spent in a deserted caravanserai.

Do you see me? Do you see where we're heading?

Tell me your secrets. You know mine.

CHAPTER TWO

HAD IT NOT BEEN for the repeated rooster cries, I would have remained asleep longer. Blue sky peeked in from the mostly missing roof of our hut. My mother called out my name; she was sitting nearby on a blanket. Next to her lay my brother, unaffected by the rooster.

The four walls bore little resemblance to those of the other two huts we had stopped at on the previous day. Bereft of color, bare, and with the sky as a ceiling, the abandoned shell brought comfort nonetheless. It was a refuge from the mountainous desert, the dry riverbed, and the palpitating sounds of invisible helicopters.

I asked about my father.

"He went for a walk. He'll be right back," she said, sounding sweet but tired as she reached for some bread and cheese. Hunger gnawing, I resigned myself to the stale breakfast graciously shared by the other mother.

Her son sat next to her, flying his cupped hand and crashing it into the ground. Reza was his name: I had heard his mother calling for him the day before. Layla lay awake beside her, occasionally passing her fingers through her long, wavy brown hair, uttering words only her mother could hear.

I wondered why, even the day before, the bread and the cheese had tasted stale. Perhaps Layla's family had been traveling longer to reach that village in Zahedan, which now seemed like long ago. "Why didn't we bring food with us, too?" I whispered to my mother.

"We were going to buy food once we reached a town. Just thought we'd reach it much sooner. Our plans changed a bit when the guard didn't let us through the border yesterday."

What I didn't know then was that the guard *hadn't* let us through, despite the money he had received from the village man to let us enter Pakistani soil.

My mother began attending to Joubin, who had awoken, helping him transition from his last memories of the night. Her comforting touch allowed for a quiet exploration of his new surroundings. Time was kind this time and gave itself freely to him.

He refused the old cheese and began chewing on his hard crust of bread. At least we have food, I thought, thanks to Layla's family.

The few words that had been exchanged between our families left all of us to silent speculation. I wondered about the life and home they had left behind. Had they had a dog? Had it been poisoned like ours?

"Where's everyone else?" I asked my mother.

"They've gone to get another truck to take us the rest of the way."

"They've gone to bring my father!" announced Reza.

Good, I thought. It made more sense that he'd be there. Why hadn't he been with them from the beginning? Where was he coming from? More questions piled onto my To Be Asked Later list.

When my father returned from his walk, we learned that he had met a village man who lived in a hut nearby who, through gesture and motion, had made it known that it was best to remain inside the hut.

"Why?" I asked.

"We're foreigners here. It'll be easier if we don't raise questions."

Why? would have been my next question, yet I was more swept by the impression that we were still not free. Had we not just passed the border? Had my father not told me we were free? Why couldn't we provide answers to this new land's questions? As I looked at the other family, it slowly sank in. I had already known that we weren't free, even before my father entered the hut. Otherwise, we would have shared our stories with the other family. We couldn't reveal our reasons for fleeing Iran, and I knew that we couldn't ask them either. Matters of the past were limited to the twenty-four hours we had shared between us.

During our wait for the others to return, I started to gain a fuller picture of the previous night.

"It was as if someone pasted a black cloth over our window," said my mother.

"I kept thinking, if we don't get caught, this driver will kill us for sure," said the other mother.

"Maheen Khanum kept whispering, '*Ya Khoda*,' every time we made a sharp turn," my mother said, drawing Maheen Khanum's laughter into her own.

"Then he says, 'We're in Pakistan.' We had to believe it— there were no signs," my mother continued.

"Imagine leaving us in that dry river of all places," said Maheen Khanum, rolling her eyes away.

That's when I learned that the raised voices I had heard were not extensions of my dreams. The driver had pleaded for the half money. He'd told us to spend the night in that riverbed and walk toward the nearby village at daybreak, insisting that he had only agreed to take us to a safe location in Pakistan. Hamid had vehemently argued that a dry riverbed did not equate with a safe drop-off point. The half money would not be returned. Nasser stayed behind with the mothers and children, while the rest set out to find another driver, which was how we found that deserted hut. That's when the half money traveled back to the village man.

"I'm happy it didn't occur to me that there might be scorpions in that riverbed," my mother added. Me too, I thought.

"Were you scared?" I asked, making both mothers turn to me.
"Not then, thank God," my mother said. "Afterward."
"Why after?" I asked.
"I don't know."

Layla did not speak much; she too must have been asleep through much of the journey. Yet her eyes were not without a voice that told me that she was near, drawing me into a smile at times.

I wondered whether she was the same age as Mina, who used to take me to her painting classes on Fridays. The walk through the busy streets of Tehran, holding my wooden box of oil paints, next to an almost-adult, had left me hungry for more autonomy: an appreciable departure from Behrooz joon's one-on-one drawing classes. My first painting had been of a vase of flowers, only it held more than the reproduced image from an old postcard. It showed me how every brush stroke produced a different possibility on the canvas, how every layer of paint introduced more meaning, how nothing is what it seems at first.

Much like everything else, our painting classes were also devoured by the Revolution.

I was happy that Layla had brought back the sensation of the oils, the smells, the textures—the hope of painting again.

"Where're we going to now?" I asked my father.

"Quetta. We need to reach a city," he began, but before he could finish his sentence and I could ask more questions, we all became alert to the distant sound of a vehicle. My father waited at the entrance until Hamid entered with a stranger. Reza's sprint

to the man with gray stubble eliminated any need for introduc-
tions. A few nods and words of greetings were sufficient. Only
minutes of rest were afforded our new travel companion.

Again, time had gained momentum, and little of it was wasted
as we quickly gathered blankets, bags, and canvases. We left the
four walls with the missing ceiling, ready to enter onto a tan pickup
truck. Different from the other trucks we had ridden in the day
before, this one contained a camper covered by canvas. Nasser appeared out of the canvas shell, and before long all the bags had been
positioned to the back of the truck bed. It seemed that, with every
transition to a new truck, we compromised on size, the latest particularly noteworthy.

Yet unlike the other times, the air was not thick with anxiety,
the faces were not as worn, and we weren't separated from my
mother and brother. I had been dreading another long journey
sitting apart from them and was thrilled to learn that, in this new
land, women couldn't sit next to male drivers. A smaller space,
and more bodies, left little room for movement, however. Shoved
together, I leaned against my father's shin, my brother on my
mother's lap.

The canvas covers were tied shut from the outside by the new
driver, blotting out the bright day.

"Why is he caging us in?" I asked my father.

"We'll be going through a long patch of dusty land," he told
me. "It's to protect us."

The driver's holler set us in motion on a new route through
the land of dust. As we powered across the barren region, the

floating soil made its way through the openings of our moving shelter and found ways into our mouths, ears, and nostrils. Cloaked in desert colors, I peeked at my father. He no longer resembled himself.

"You're blonde," I informed him and immediately regretted allowing more graininess to enter my mouth.

He peered through his dusty lashes and smiled in response. What would we have looked like without the canvas shell, which equally served as means to escape the fierce sun?

My eyes closed, I could only see orange, taste sand, hear the engine, give in to the heat, and ignore the bruises from the uneven pathways.

Long hours passed within our enclosed space amid silent thoughts and day dreams momentarily interrupted by one of our bodies needing to reposition itself. Squinting determined the levels of adjustment required for the new configuration. Once adapted, we would return to our internal voices, sightless and without speech.

My mind drifted in all directions, and I followed. In my wandering, I was brought home, to our backyard, in the middle of winter. Joubin and I had been celebrating the newly fallen snow by building a snowman. With pebbles for its eyes, my borrowed hat and Joubin's mittens, the snowman had called for a nose. In our excitement we rang our neighbor's home, because his door was steps closer than our own from our shared back yard. Old Mr. Shamimi answered our call and searched for a carrot in his kitchen. He offered one with many apologies for not having more.

"We only need one," we assured him.

Ready to add the final touch, we hurried back to our snowman. To celebrate we returned to Mr. Shamimi's for a cup of hot chocolate, as we often did.

Mrs. Shamimi had just come home from the markets and embraced us in her usual bright manner. Her husband grabbed her shopping bags and headed towards their kitchen.

"Oh, you found carrots!" he said from a distance. "I thought their mother needed carrots for soup, so I gave them our last one, and then from the window I see them sticking it into a snowman."

We all laughed and sipped more of the cocoa he had made.

What would have happened if there hadn't been any carrots at the market that day? I wondered. It wouldn't have been unusual. Would Mr. Shamimi have reclaimed the last carrot from our snowman? He wouldn't have. It wouldn't have mattered to Joubin and me; we weren't blind to the long queues for food and gas. Nonetheless, it wouldn't have been something he would've done. Of that I was sure and continued to sip cocoa. It had never tasted better.

"WE'RE TAKING A BREAK," said Hamid when our truck slowed down. *Finally*, I thought. We came to a halt. Bright rays of light flooded in as the driver opened the canvas door. I pictured us all hopping down to relieve our painful bodies. My tailbone was completely numb. It had transferred its throbbing towards my abdomen at some point during our journey. When it came time to lift our bodies to descend, I could barely move. Fresh pain prevented my knees from unfolding at first. None of us could stand straight. When our feet eventually reached the dusty ground, we saw that we had arrived at a checkpoint in a makeshift area. Several other trucks had stopped there as well, for routine inspections and rest. Men in *shalvar khamis* and long vests were scattered around, few of them with families. I guess the women wear veils here as well, I said to myself. At least here they don't wear them tight around their faces like we were forced to do back home. As we shook the dust from our clothing, Nasser handed us bowls of warm yellow split peas and bread. I hadn't even noticed him leave our group.

Grateful, my parents handed Joubin and me pieces of bread, which we consumed immediately. The golden stew reminded me of the pencil drawings of porridge from my brother's *Goldilocks* picture book. With no spoons at hand, we dipped our bread into the split peas and took a bite.

A violent attack of spices brought tears flowing from our eyes and noses, and we were barely able to swallow what had seemed like heavenly food seconds before. My parents quickly tasted the split peas. The fire even challenged their spice threshold. With raised brows, they tried to comfort us, and the bread was our only relief. It was not stale and calmed our burning tongues. I stared at Hamid and Nasser, who showed no sign of discomfort in eating their meal.

"They're used to Pakistani chili peppers," my father explained—a statement well beyond my reach. My mother handed us water, which Joubin and I drank reluctantly. We couldn't stomach the water we'd been carrying with us from the beginning of our journey. It smelled like a farm and tasted like it had been dead, yet apparently Hamid preferred it to the water that was available at our stop.

My parents managed to finish their shared bowl of what we came to know as *dhal*; they no longer sensed their smoldering mouths anyway. Nasser's discreet signal to us indicated the end of our temporary relief from the repeated bruisings, the stale air of sweat, and the tight, confined space.

"But we just got here," Reza protested. Accompanied by his bawling, we climbed into the truck. My father sat in his earlier position. The pangs from my tailbone returned, but there wasn't much time or space to rethink our positions.

The heat was unforgiving, the dry earth relentless, the truck wild. Locked in an orange world behind my closed lids, I welcomed the images from home that played before me. I heard from a time where all my friends were together—the Germans, the Iranians, the ones that were both—a time we had spent playing endless games of *lay-lay*, *kesh-bazi*, and *tanab-bazi*, sharing custard-filled *peerashkis* and Chiclets. The brown paste under our fingernails told of our grimaces from the brutally sour *tambreh hendi*; orange fingers were a clear give-away of *Poffak Namaki*; the eggplant color around our cuticles spoke of the juicy sweet and sour *albaloo khoshkeh*, and the sticky fingers were usually linked to plum or pomegranate *lavashak*.

A LOUD BANGING TORE through our silent worlds. The noise came from the driver's direction, a hammering against the metal frame.

"We're coming to a checkpoint!" yelled Hamid. I didn't have to prepare much for my sleeping role, as I hadn't opened my eyes for hours. Instead, I leaned further into my father's shins and repeated my line to myself: *My name is Golbakht.* Surely, these guards would be better than the one on the previous day. I made sure that I believed that.

Within minutes, our truck came to a halt. I guessed that our canvas shell had been opened, for bright streaks of orange suddenly broke through the darker shades that had accompanied me for hours. Hamid and Nasser's voices leaped out of the truck, intermingled with other male voices in a different foreign tongue; nothing seemed familiar.

Suddenly, a strange voice demanded something in our direction in English. "Yes, yes," answered the other father in a seeming attempt to descend, continuing his response in the same tongue.

The "yes, yes," quickly followed by "no! no! no!" were among the few words I knew in English and offered no insight to what was occurring on the ground. *Pakistan* was the one other word I understood.

The incessant heat seemed to double the time we spent at the checkpoint. After what seemed longer than fifteen minutes but less than an hour, we were charging through the desert sand again, back to our inner voices, and I back to my friends—to the ballet class some of us attended. We loved our ballet teacher and wanted to be like her in as many ways as possible. Her tall, graceful body made the *pliés* and twirls seem easy, yet somehow my body never reached the flexibility my friends shared. Even so, I loved dancing, especially with Ghazal, Leili, and Bita. From the wooden benches in the studio, our mothers watched us dance, waiting patiently, as did the soggy tomato-and-pickled-egg sandwiches that I had grown to dislike. It keeps, and it's protein, I had learned.

In that truck, breathing in our sticky bodies, I would have given anything for a smelly egg sandwich.

Hours later, the thumping signal from the driver didn't precede the slowing of our truck. Another checkpoint? No sound came from Hamid, so I had to hold on to my questions longer.

"Let's get down," my father whispered once we stopped. Finally daring to squint, I saw a thin layer of desert gold covering our entire bodies. I had grown tired of the taste of earth. I wasn't at first even concerned about why we were to descend; it meant relief for our entangled bodies, if only for a few minutes. In the back corner, I saw my mother caressing my brother awake. Both boys were deep asleep in their mother's arms.

Moments later, the driver's assistant untied the camper covering and we proceeded to release ourselves from our crouched molds. Once we landed on dry ground, however, our stiff muscles and achy bones were overshadowed by the view of a tea house that stood alone in the distance, surrounded by dry barren desert and, here and there, desiccated shrubs.

Hamid and Nasser threw the rough canvas covers to the ground, and the fathers helped to spread them out. Though meant to be sat on, no one went near them. Upright, our eyes followed Hamid and the driver to the run-down building. At last one of my wishes was fulfilled when I saw them returning with trays in their hands, hoping that the food and water wasn't going to smell or taste rancid or fiery.

The trays of bread, *dhal*, and a kettle with cups were placed onto the canvas by Nasser and Hamid, magnetizing us all around them. Hot water in this heat? I wondered before I saw Reza's father, Javeed Agha, pour milky tea from the kettle.

"Oh, it's sweet tea," noted my mother, sipping.

"It's called *doodh patti*", explained Nasser, nodding. "It's Pakistani tea. *Doodh* means milk. *Patti* are leaves, tea leaves."

"There's cardamom in it, too," she remarked.

"They make it with *chai*, milk, sugar, and cardamom," said Javeed Agha. "They boil water in a pot, put in cardamom first, then the sugar, then the *chai* and then let 'em all boil together. That's when they add a lot of milk, so it's more milk than tea."

"*Naan* and *chai*," our mother said to Joubin and me as she handed us the pieces of bread.

I was relishing their words about tea—not because they were about tea, but because there were *words* again, words that had nothing to do with murmured plans. It was heavenly, the *doodh patti*, the *naan*, the freedom to move our limbs. It didn't even matter that I'd always disliked cardamom, or that we were wet from an entire day spent in a baking tin on the move. I breathed in every word.

"Javeed Agha says to the guard, 'I'm a resident of Pakistan'," Nasser said, recounting the last phrase in English. "Then the guard asks, 'The President of Pakistan?' and he quickly says, 'No, no, no. A resident! A *resident!*'"

Everyone laughed. "What did he just say?" I whispered to my mother, who quickly translated Nasser's words.

Dusk brought release from the bondage of heat. My father chased Reza, Joubin, and me in a game of tag. He was much slower in catching us than usual, his movements strained and sluggish. We ran, laughed, and panted.

"We'll have to spend the night here," Hamid announced when we rejoined the group.

"Good!" exclaimed my father. "It's a beautiful night!"

"Women and children in the truck, the men on the ground," continued Hamid, not as enthusiastic as my father to be spending the night in the open cold.

Hours before, we had barely been able to breathe in the hot air; now we were shivering in our coats. My mother and Maheen Khanum handed several blankets and bags from the truck to Nasser in preparation for a night to be spent in the middle of a land with nothing in sight but the shadows of a remote tea house, distant mountains, and a star-packed sky that seemed different from the previous night's—free of invisible lines, void of calculated moves around a guard's tea break, though apparently not un-bounded by a much-discussed checkpoint we were to face the fol-lowing day.

Our mothers called out to their husbands to bring their sons to them after they had transformed the interior of the truck to a sleeping room. I wasn't ready to let go of the collective words just yet, and I used my four-year-and-four-month advantage over my brother to stay up a little while longer. My father had begun a tale about a famous philosopher, who was also a poet and a scholar, and I wanted to hear it to the end.

"On one of his journeys, he stops at a tea house one night. It was a beautiful night, clear and fresh, so he asks the owner of the tea house to spread his cot outside. The owner tells him that his dog always spends the nights outside and only chooses to come in on the nights that carry midnight rain. This particular night, his dog had come inside to sleep; hence there would be rain. The famous scholar studied the sky and said, 'There is no chance that it'll rain. The skies are as clear as I've ever seen them.' The owner shrugged and did as the scholar demanded.

"Well, it poured that night! The scholar, soaking wet, knocked on the door of the tea house and told the owner, 'I wanted to let you know that your dog has more knowledge than me.'"

Everyone laughed, most of all my father, who always laughs first at his own jokes.

"Well, we're in trouble tonight then," chuckled Nasser, "'cause I don't see any dogs or other animals around here!"

The jokes and laughter carried us into the hours of the night under the tightly clustered stars.

"Time to sleep," my mother said to me. Reluctantly, I lifted myself from the ground. But there would be more stories I would miss, words and humor sure to be lost the following day, which was to contain more dust-filled hours under a brutal sun.

"What if it rains on them tonight?" I asked my mother when we entered our sleeping abode in the truck.

"It won't," my mother said, holding my shoulder gently. "That

."

if it does?"

not a cloud in sight. The story was just to make everyone laugh."

It had made everyone laugh, even Hamid, as had Nasser's re-counting of other encounters at the checkpoint earlier that day. That's when I had learned that, other than our fake Afghan pass-ports, Hamid had passed down the same three bags for inspection, one at a time. The guards never realized that they were checking the same three bags in rotation, saving us from possible questions. What were a group of Afghan and Pakistani villagers doing with bags filled with western clothing?

My mother didn't head back to the night's conversations. She lay beside Joubin and me and covered us with a blanket. Cuddled against her, I listened to the faint voices that were no longer laugh-ing.

I caught a corner of the moon through the slit of the canvas shell above me. Somewhere between its magnetic pull and the dis-tant murmurs, I fell asleep.

> *The moon shines*
> *With its gentle touch*
> *It smiles*
> *And I'm not alone.*

In the early hours of the morning, we were awakened to the sounds of Hamid's and Nasser's voices speaking in a foreign tongue.

Someone had already laid out breakfast on the canvas sheet on the ground. Joubin and Reza sipped their *doodh patti*, sitting on their mother's lap. Free at last from our own stale bread and cheese, we relished our meal beneath the hints of the rising sun.

Our driver shouted words from a distance, and Hamid acknowledged him by raising his hand.

"We need to hurry. We want to get ahead as far as possible before it gets too hot," he told us.

I'd forgotten about the driver and his assistant until then. Where had they been last night? Where had they slept?

Layla and I sat next to each other, sipping our teas and chewing our flat bread. She and Maheen Khanum had stayed up late with the others. I envied the extra accounts Layla'd been privy to and was to take with her on our next blind and wordless stretch forward.

"When we stop, the kids don't have to pretend to sleep anymore. They won't ask them anything," Hamid informed our parents. "But they absolutely can't say a word!" he added, looking at Reza's parents. All nodded in response to his weighty yet quiet voice.

Time did not flow as naturally as it had the night before. In haste, Nasser and Hamid repositioned our bags, canvas sheets, bread, and water inside the truck. Our rested bodies curled back to the fetal positions of the previous day, surrendering to the inescapable heat and bruisings that were to accompany us through our third day in the desert. Obliged that the sun's full force had not as yet penetrated the earth, we sped across the arid ground at full speed, blasting the dust through the air, a disturbance repaid by the vengeful particles that found ways to crawl into our senses, settling into our nostrils, our ears, our mouths. Closing my lids tightly, I fought off the grains that perched unto my lashes. Back to my mute world, seeing nothing but vague orange shadows, I sought out Ariane, my friend from school. I had sat next to her in class, shared stories from home with her, along with any delicious treats that would make our mouths water. I missed her more than ever. Our last conversation played itself in front of me over and over, like a bad dream.

AFTER MANY REPEATED PLEAS, my mother had finally granted me one phone call to Ariane, but not before I received careful instructions on what was not to be said in the bugged conversation. It was common knowledge that the telephone lines were monitored throughout the country. I had loved overhearing afternoon chats, over fruits and *chaee*, about codes and signals people created to relay messages in their surveilled phone conversations.

"Where have you *been?*" Ariane had asked.

"How are Ghazal and Leili?" I'd asked, happy to finally be in touch again.

"It's been two weeks!"

"How are things going at school? How are Bita, Parvaneh, and Sheila?"

"Fine. You know, the same stuff. Khanumeh Hakim is still as mean as before. Actually, I think she's become even meaner. She's always snapping at us."

How's the business going?" I'd asked, referring to the bead-making business that I had accidentally started. Somehow I had stumbled upon it one day when I brought a few beaded pins and bracelets to school. Surrounded by my classmates, custom-made orders started coming in from every direction. Unable to meet the demand, Ariane had helped collect and make the orders as well— thus, the beginning of our partnership.

"Oh, it's great! We have these new designs now. We can barely get to all the orders. We're staying up late after our homework, just to keep up."

"Who is *we*?"

"Gissou and I," she had said. "You should see the new patterns she's come up with. They're really pretty."

"I can't!"

"You can't what?"

"See the patterns!" I'd said with an edge to my voice.

"Oh, it's blue, yellow, blue, yellow, then three reds, then blue, yellow, blue, yellow again. Why can't you come and see them?"

"I'm surprised you didn't go with lime green instead of the blue. It's much more 'chic'!" I'd said.

"There's another version, with different colors, purple—"

"What about the navy-and-white design? Is that still a favorite?"

"Well, everyone *bought* that from us already, so we had to come up with new ones. We're thinking of doing anklets next."

"Why would you want to do anklets, if we can't even show our feet?" I had asked, trying hard to control my voice.

"Well, we can wear them at home," she'd answered with a chuckle.

What's so funny? I had wondered, but I'd known why she was laughing. It made me feel like I was my brother's playmate. Words and humor had always flowed easily between Ariane and me, until that phone call. We'd been a team— not just us, our entire class. Initially, this camaraderie had been born of the endless games of *estop rangui*, of singing German rhymes to hand-clapping games, of sharing potato chips that came in long, clear bags, the sugar buzz from dipping our fingers into Kool-Aid powder. It had come from debating whether to heed our mothers' warnings about buying *chaghaleh badoom* or *gojeh sabz* from the street vendors, who washed the fruits with water from the *joob* and artfully coned them into newspaper.

"I gotta go. Take care of yourself!" I'd said quickly.

Ariane had mumbled something back in confusion.

"All right. Have fun with the beads," I had added airily.

Click.

I had stormed into our playroom, where Joubin was playing with his toy airplanes and Legos.

"You wanna play? Look at my airport," he had said proudly.

"No," I'd grumbled.

I had climbed behind the cardboard store we'd built together. But then my questions had followed me to the store, pestering me. *What was she supposed to do? Did you know your business would turn into an enterprise? Would you have done any differently? Go away!* I said to the voice in my head, leaving me sitting by my cardboard box, staring down at the hand-written price tags on our toys, made ready to belong to other kids. There had been hardly any occasions to sell much, but we'd kept "the shop" open just in case. Things weren't moving as fast as they had the first time we had put our belongings for sale. That had been a year before—our first attempt to leave Iran—before Iraq bombed Iran's airport.

The day before our scheduled flight to Germany, our living room had been packed with a dozen people, each holding one of our household items ready to be purchased.

Then the telephone had rung. It was my father.

"They've just bombed the airport!"

"Stop!" my mother had shouted, still holding the receiver. "Excuse me, everyone! Stop! Nothing is on sale anymore!"

We had spent the following weeks buying domestic essentials, as most things had already been sold.

BY THE LATE MORNING hours, we were well into the desert heat. Thanks to my father's shins, my back, though sore, was in far less agony than my tailbone. I could barely continue to sit yet had no alternative but to bear my weight longer on the pain.

The driver's pounding signal from the front foretold an upcoming checkpoint. Perhaps this time they would ask us to descend from the truck. All I wanted to do was drop to the ground and have someone roll out my limbs like dough on flour dust.

"We're stopping at the checkpoint," Hamid confirmed. "No one speaks!"

Then I heard him spit, and I wanted to do the same. My internal grinding noises had become louder than the engine for me. I rested my hopes on spitting out the grains at the checkpoint we were nearing.

Unlike the other times, I didn't have to remain trapped behind my closed lids once we stopped. Hamid, Nasser, and Reza's father, Javeed Agha, descended with our passports in hand and were almost immediately in dialogue with the officers. Whatever our crew communicated to the guards, it allowed little room for response in return. With three bodies out of the truck, we all shifted our limbs as much as we could. I turned to my father and pointed to my mouth. He handed me a tissue and I spat out the graininess. When would they tell us to come out of the truck? I shifted my weight slightly to my side, desperate to stretch out. Instead, we remained in that position after our three men returned to the truck.

Before the sand lifted too high off the ground from the acceleration, Nasser shouted: "The next checkpoint is the big one."

My name is Golbakht, I said to myself. *Maybe they won't even ask my name*, I thought quickly. I wished I could ask when we'd reach the checkpoint, but I'd just spat out some dust and wasn't about to let in any more.

Packed with nine other people, I felt alone, with only my thoughts as my companions. I was tired of thinking about Ariane. I was tired of missing her and everyone else at home. At the same time, I was relieved not to spend hours playing in our homemade store empty of customers, grateful for not having to stay in our darkened home, draped with thick curtains, with windows covered in black paper as mandated by the war. Not a glimmer of light was to be seen from any home, in case Iraqi bombers flew over us. On a dark night, not a streetlight was to be seen, not a headlight, not even the light of a cigarette. Though bleak, it had proved fun on one occasion. Piled in a car with family friends, we had all tried to reach their home before dark. Traffic had caused delays, and darkness was a stone's throw away.

Minutes from their home, we could see nothing but shadows. Without headlights, it was impossible to determine which streets we were passing. To avoid collision with other moving cars, we rolled down all our windows, relying on sounds to direct us. Guided by honks and shouts, we inched our way through. My mother's friend, Jinus, waved her entire arm out of the passenger window.

"Come on, Khandan. Do the same," she said.

"What are you doing?" her husband Farhad asked.

"Waving our arms to make sure we don't pass against something too closely," Jinus responded.

"I think you need to wave from the front of the car, not the side," her husband joked.

I missed our times together. Their older daughter, Maryam, was a year older than I was, and their Neda was a year older than Joubin. We had become quite close from the many hours our families spent together, the endless dinners, games of *takhteh*, and taking refuge during bomb raids. We had been together during Tehran's first bombing. That afternoon, Maryam and I had watched a television program that introduced us, for the first time, to the sound of a bomb siren. We didn't think much of it until that night, while we were playing *takhteh*.

"Isn't that the sound we heard on TV?" asked Maryam.

We drew the curtains from her bedroom window and looked out in disbelief. Flashing white and red lights filled the sky.

"Mommy! *Maman! Babí! Baba!*" Our screams brought our parents flying into our room, their alarmed questions instantly ceasing at the sight of the battle in the sky.

"Come!" Farhad shouted. "To the basement!"

My mother grabbed my hand, and in a flash we were following Farhad to the balcony, my father and Joubin steps behind. In the open air, we were under massive flurries of flares. Red flames dropping, white streaks surging, mixed with outbursts of sound I had only heard in war movies or at fireworks.

"Be careful in the dark!" screamed Jinus, leading us down their spiral fire escape.

In our haste, Joubin's sandal became stuck in one of the iron steps. My father crouched down over him to release his little foot as my mother and I stood frozen, watching from midway down the stairwell.

"Hurry!" Farhad urged from below.

Neda's crying mounted toward us.

"It's out. Keep moving!" my father called out.

We held on tight to the railings of the shaky stairwell, hurling us further into a whirlwind of panic. Once on the ground, in their garden, we ran toward a door.

"It's very dark! Be careful!" shouted Jinus over Neda's shrieking.

We could barely see the shadows of steps leading us down to their basement. Slowly feeling our way down, we all at last found ourselves standing together in the middle of the cement room.

"It's gonna *hit* us!" Neda screamed.

"*No, it's not!*" Jinus exclaimed even more loudly.

"It's far from us!" said Farhad.

How had we not heard these explosions from the house? Our music couldn't have been playing that loud. We knew how low to set it, so it couldn't be heard from the outside. Had it just started when we heard the siren? Where were my grandparents hiding? They didn't have a basement. Was my grandmother crying? Were my friends all right? Were their homes being destroyed? How far away were the fires?

Amid Neda's inconsolable wailing, we watched the war of lights from a tiny window in our shelter below the ground.

From that night onward, bomb sirens, evacuations, and bomb shelters became part of life. If we were at school during a bomb raid, we'd be walked out of our building to stand against the ground walls; if at home, we'd come out into our garden. On one such occasion, Mrs. Shamimi had joined us by the pool, wearing a baby blue floral gown and red lipstick.

"Oh, you're looking fancy, Khanumeh Shamimi. Were you expecting guests?" my mother had asked.

"Oh, no, dear," she chuckled. "Just thought, if I'm gonna die now, I might as well die pretty."

I loved her.

Bomb sirens had invaded our lives on a regular basis. I knew the routine: Assemble and move to safety. Yet on the day that my father and I were driving Maryam back to her house, the sirens hadn't steered me to action. A Pasdar stopped our car and told all within his vicinity to take refuge against any wall. My father had moved us towards the tall facade of a home. I could not take my gaze away from the planes, could not stop my body from shaking. Maryam had called out my name several times. I could hear her over the sounds of the planes and explosions, but couldn't tear my eyes away from the streaks of white smoke that were flashing up from the ground. What had broken my vision was my father's tall body in front of me, holding me by the shoulders, calling my name, and saying all was going to be fine. I'd heard him, seen him, but couldn't stop shaking.

"THIS IS IT," SAID Hamid. "It's the big one."

The moment our truck came to a full stop, Hamid and Nasser jumped down to the ground. We could hear their voices speaking the local dialect with another male voice. Hamid drew back the canvas cover.

"Sleep!" he said to us kids in a low, firm voice as he reached for the bag that lay by the edge of the truck for inspection. "They want to search inside."

As with the other times, Hamid's and Nasser's voices left little room for the other guards to be heard. In the midst of their loud discussions, we heard the voice of a woman. Her struggle to climb onto the rear load of our truck gave my mother the minute she needed to grab our Iranian passports from a nearby bag and sit on them. Hamid was holding our fake Afghan passports in his hand. No other guard had come into our truck until then. Hamid climbed in behind the female guard and sat next to Layla, who was first to be body-searched by the female guard. She played her sleeping role to the fullest. Regardless of how she was flipped by the guard, she did not *wake up,* until the guard reached her mother, who had started to become agitated by the search. Her bewildered cries made us forget our sleep instructions. All I saw was a female guard, wearing a *shalvar khamis* with a sweater and a badge, holding Maheen Khanum's gold chain, which she had been hiding around her neck. Prized rings and pendants dangled from the necklace, causing the guard's shrill voice to bounce around our enclosed space. I looked to my parents, but they seemed as taken aback as us kids. Both women were screaming. Why wasn't someone doing something? Suddenly, I felt a cold, wet slime on my left hand. Cream? I wondered, as I looked down and saw Hamid continuing on to daub more white paste on Joubin's hand. Has he gone cuckoo? I thought in my panic.

"Rub!" he said calmly, and continued to smear Nivea cream on my mother's, father's, and Layla's hands. Nothing was making sense, least of all Hamid's outrageous urge to relieve us all of dry skin in the midst of all the uproar. Completely unfazed by the outcries and distress, he applied some to his own palm, then to the guard's hands as well as the screaming Maheen Khanum's.

Everyone, and everything, stopped. Hamid leaned back against the truck, serene and unperturbed, and began rubbing his hands together as if he was sitting by a pool. He said something to the guard in her dialect, and she began to rub her hands together as well, just as perplexed as the rest of us. Nasser leapt on the precious and strange moment. He called out to the guard, from where he was standing outside, seemingly complaining about a situation to do with the first guard. His frustrated ramblings allowed Hamid, by then on the ground, to join in on the upheaval; but this time, Javeed Agha stayed out of it. He remained still in his spot. His face looked different, pale and washed out. Somehow, Nasser and Hamid had managed to shift the guards' attention away from the necklace to matters of greater import. Whatever it was, we were en route not long after.

"What were you thinking, wearing your jewels around your neck?" Hamid's voice thundered throughout the truck.

Before she had a chance to respond, her husband's voice clamored over Hamid's. "They could have arrested us!" he shouted at her. "This could've been our end!"

"What do we have *left* outside of these jewels?" she burst out.

Four big suitcases, I thought silently. This was before I knew that my father had sewn thin sticks of gold inside his belt.

This time it seemed that it was much more than the dust that kept us all quiet for hours. I couldn't find reason or logic to anything that was happening. Why could this have been our end? How did Nivea cream end up saving us? When would we be free? In Quetta? It had to be.

I wanted to cry. The pain in my tailbone was becoming intolerable. How was it that I could be both numb and ache, in the same spot, simultaneously?

By sundown, I felt as if my internal cries had been heard when I could finally make out other engines, the honking of mini buses, and people's voices. We had reached a town. We had at last reached Quetta.

"Where're we going now?" Joubin, barely audible, asked our mother.

"The hotel," she answered.

Yes! I thought. The hotel. The lounge. Though it had only been two nights since we left Iran, it seemed as if we had been in the desert for a week. It didn't matter anymore. We were minutes away from the hotel and my cup of cocoa.

It took more than a few minutes to straighten our sore limbs and spines as we adjusted to an upright position in the truck.

"They're gonna know we're runaways if we all go in at the same time," said Hamid. "Nasser and I will go in first to get the keys to the rooms. Javeed Agha, you follow in five minutes. The rest of you stay in here 'til we come for you."

It didn't take long before Nasser returned. "We're all on the second floor. They'll heat water and bring it to you," said Nasser to my father as he handed him our key. "Head straight to your room. Don't look around too much. We want as little attention as possible."

To Maheen Khanum he added, "Javeed Agha will come out in a few minutes. You'll go in with him."

"What are you looking for?" Joubin asked me.

"The hotel," I said when we were nearing an untended building with gated windows.

Per Nasser's directives, Joubin, my mother, and I followed my father towards our room—not too fast, not too slow, not too escapee looking, not too anything.

Our room consisted of two beds, a dresser, an old lamp, and a bathroom. Who cared about cocoa? It was our own private haven, far surpassing sleeping in a truck, a ceilingless hut, or an arid desert that seemed to stretch to no end.

"I have to go to the bathroom," said Joubin, fidgeting about.

"Come," said our mother, directing him to the bathroom. "Don't touch anything!"

"Yes, aim from a meter away," said my father, a running joke we had with our mother anytime we were remotely close to a hotel toilet.

"This is a bathroom?" asked Joubin. "It has a *stage* in it."

"What?" I asked, and walked in to see. "Oh, it's true!"

We were standing in a gray cement room with a big drain in the middle of the floor, and a platform on one side. The sink and toilet almost looked out of place. Fortunately for our mother, she wouldn't need to disinfect anything, since it was one of those squat toilets—a bonus, since we didn't carry disinfectants.

"Oh, good," she said upon seeing our father enter our giant shower with a couple of old faded buckets. "The water is ready."

"What's it for?" asked Joubin.

"To bathe. Come on, let's take off these clothes."

"We're *all* gonna go in the buckets?"

"No, we'll use the bowl to pour the water over us," my mother said with a laugh.

"We're throwing our clothes on the ground?" I asked in disbelief after seeing her toss Joubin's clothes in a mold-covered corner.

"We won't be wearing these clothes again," she said as she threw my clothes on top of the dusty pile. "And they're filthy, so let's leave them on the ground."

She scooped out the hot water, filling the bowl half way, then mixed in some cold water from the other bucket to pour over our heads. The precious warm drizzle ran through my hair, my scalp, and face. Even with the sparse splashes of water that never seemed to fully cover my entire body, I could not recall when it felt so rejuvenating to bathe, every sprinkle a soothing balm against my face, a sense of cleanness I had almost forgotten. It took many washings before the dribbling water from my body ran clear of the cloudy dust that had latched on to me for so long.

Our father had laid out our fresh clothes on our beds. I raced to my navy corduroys and cream cotton top, the same clothes we had worn on the plane to Zahedan.

Our parents each took turns bathing, while the other sat with us on the bed, mostly answering our questions:

"How long will we stay here?"

"Just tonight."

"Do we have to ride the truck again?"

"No. We're going to fly!"

"Another airplane!" Joubin said, sitting up on the bed.

"Where?" I asked.

"To Lahore. It's another city in Pakistan."

"Do they have a hotel there?" I wondered as Joubin asked his next question: "Is that where *Shomal* is?"

"Listen, Mommy and I want to say something to both of you," he said, when my mother was ready. He wore the face that usually foretold a lengthy discussion. "We want you to know that we've noticed how patient you've been during our trip," he said, making sure every word was being heard. "The ride in the truck was long. We know it wasn't easy."

"Neither one of you've complained ever since we left Tehran," our mother added.

"Thank you," said my father.

I had been expecting to hear a detailed explanation about the city of Lahore, some way out of Joubin's expectation of playing in the waves up north. It wasn't out of character for our parents to recognize and acknowledge virtues, yet somehow, there and then, receiving such praise surprised me. There had been no other choice, I thought to say, but instead only responded with a beaming smile, taking their words to a place inside me where I knew I could find them in case I needed them.

"Let's go eat!" said my father, after Joubin and I had received the final strokes of their praise and embrace. "I'm sure everyone's waiting."

Until he mentioned "everyone," I realized, I hadn't thought about the rest of our travel companions since we entered our room.

"Where are they waiting?" asked our mother.

"In Hamid's room," he replied.

Across the inner courtyard, we were the last to join our companions, who were already sitting around a white tablecloth spread on Hamid's floor. Bowls of *dhal*, spicy potato stew, yogurt, *naan*, and *doodh patti* sat in the middle.

Joubin and I devoured the *naan* and yogurt on our plates. What would have usually taken him an hour to eat, he polished off in minutes. After every bite of my *naan*, I took in the whiff of glycerin soap that still lingered on my hands, a welcome change from the scent of sweat we had carried for two long days. Like a bunch of onions whose wilted and moldy outer layers had just been peeled off, we ate, talked, and laughed.

"What in the world made you think to put cream on us at that moment?" my father asked Hamid.

"It worked, didn't it?" he replied, with a half smile.

"Yes, but how did you know it was going to?"

"I didn't. I just wanted to give off an air that we weren't panicking."

"Well, it freed us from her," Nasser said nodding.

Free from "her," free from Golbakht, from one another's pressed bodies, and from whatever had brought us all together in Quetta, within the four plain walls of murky white.

We still had to reach Lahore, but that was for tomorrow. Tonight was reserved for a restful sleep, in beds.

CHAPTER THREE

I REVELED IN THE SCENT of eggs, *naan* and *doodh patti* that permeated Hamid's room the next day, instantly taking me back home, to the delightful breakfasts I had always thought were the best qualities of a morning. I liked them so much that I would at times have three breakfasts in one morning on the days that I spent at Pari joon's, when she and my grandfather, Abbas joon, still lived in Tehran. The *noon barbari, panir Irani,* and *chaee* I would enjoy with Pari joon, sitting face-to-face around her beautifully set table, covered with a white tablecloth, with flowers from their garden as its centerpiece. I'd set aside my pre-sliced cantaloupe and halved pink grapefruit for my second breakfast with Abbas joon, eagerly awaiting his arrival, pre-announced by the inviting scent of his aftershave as he descended the stairway. Then I'd await his bright and lively *"Bahh-bahh! Roya janeh gol!"* Like all who were loved by him, I'd receive his tight hugs and would be passionately tapped like a drum, enjoying the sound of the beats and rhythms on my back, sinking further into his freshly pressed dress shirt and tie, inhaling his cologne, and looking forward to our breakfast together, giggling as he showered Pari joon with adorations and love. It was a love that pulled anyone within its vicinity into its magnetic hold.

By mid morning, it would be time for my third breakfast, "Akhtar" style. She was one of my grandparents' beloved house-keepers.

"How come you always have your breakfasts on a sheet on the ground?" I had asked her one day, as I joined her for our usual *noon barbari, panir Irani,* and *chaee* together.

"I'm from the village, Nanneh joon. And it's more comfort-able, isn't it?" she asked me, her thick feet sticking out of her light blue cotton dress.

I nodded supportively as I sipped my *chaee* the way she did, from the saucer. Akhtar poured more tea from her clear little sil-houette-shaped glass into her deep saucers to cool it down faster. It was a tea-drinking method I had often observed among stubbly men in their stores or nearby *Chaee Khanehs.*

THE NEW DAY CAST its reflection on all our faces. I could see it—not so much in what was visible, but in what was absent, like the lines on Javeed Agha's forehead, the silence that had forced us into ourselves, the tension that had masked our voices, and Hamid's piercing eyes, from which there was little chance of escaping, even though they'd been mostly directed off into space.

"What time do we leave?" asked my father.

"Fifteen minutes," Nasser answered after a sip of his tea.

"Where're we going?" asked Reza with interest.

"You're staying here with your mother. We'll be back later," answered his father.

"Are you going, too?" I whispered to my father.

"We're going to buy the plane tickets to Lahore and to Germany," he whispered with a nod and smiling eyes.

My eyes widened. "Germany?" I asked brightly.

That's where we were heading all along, I thought to myself. Plane tickets to Germany, I said to myself. Could we really be hours away from being lifted off to another life? Then we'd be really free.

I chewed on my *naan* and dreamed about my cousins we would soon be reunited with in Germany. Schabi and I were going to play records, dip cookies in our teas, and play with my little cousin, who was just a toddler. My dreams continued even after the men in our group left to buy the plane tickets.

Joubin and Reza passed the little Hot Wheels back and forth between them; their mothers packed up the leftover eggs and *naan*, and their sisters were somewhere far in another place and time.

Midway through my reverie, Hamid entered the room with the rest of the men steps behind. Why doesn't he look like this morning anymore? I wondered when I saw him. The heaviness in his gaze was back. It's over now! I wanted to tell him.

"Change of plans," said Javeed Agha. His forehead was once

again inflicted with lines.

"What happened?" asked Maheen Khanum in her usual nervous tone.

"They're all over the airport, and security is tight," he answered, rubbing his gray stubble.

"Will we drive there then?" asked my mother.

"That would take a few days, and the route won't be easy. We'll have to take the train," concluded Hamid, whose words I wanted to embrace. The thought of another ride in a truck felt like signing up for a tumble in a packed clothes dryer.

"They won't check for passports there?" asked Maheen Khanum.

"Not as thoroughly as in the airport," Javeed Agha answered.

"When we reach the guard, walk behind Hamid and me," said Nasser to my father. "Let's pray they won't ask for your passports."

"We'll go now to buy all our train tickets, since our passports are valid," said Hamid, referring to Nasser, Javeed Agha, and himself.

"When we return, your family will leave the inn first," he said to Javeed Agha. "The rest of us will follow three minutes later."

A nod from Javeed Agha set everything in motion: The ticket buyers left, and my family returned to our room. A train, I thought as I sat on our bed. Had I been on a train before? I wondered. I remembered riding *Strassenbahns* in Vienna, but not locomotive trains. Scenes from my favorite Czech black-and-white film, *Train in the Snow*, flashed before me, one of a handful of non-war films that hadn't been banned from television in Iran. Every time it aired, I thanked God that the Islamic Revolution didn't consider a Czech film about some stranded school kids on a train during a snow blizzard a threat to Islamic values.

My father was flooded with Joubin's questions about trains, as he zipped up our little bags. How big was the train going to be? How many cars? How long would the ride take? Would there be a whistle? And my father enthusiastically answered every question. My mother was quiet, in a distant place we knew needed to be visited only by herself.

A train ride to a plane to Germany seemed like an exciting adventure. As it happened, the adventure began before we even left our room, when it dawned on my mother that we would still have to blend in somewhat on the train, which meant we would have to wear the same filthy and sweaty clothes we had thrown in the bathroom corner the night before. They had remained on the floor, thought of as trash. Upon seeing her face as she was dressing Joubin, one would have thought that she had been forced to smear frog slime all over his body. I suppose she wasn't far off.

A *tap-tap tap tap-tap* on our door let my father know that Hamid was on the other side. He quickly let him and Nasser into our room.

"When do we leave?" my mother asked after my father shut the door.

"Now," Hamid said quickly. "The train leaves in an hour. We'll reach Lahore tomorrow around six in the evening. There's only one train a day to Lahore, so they better not give us any hassles. The rest just left, so we have to move right now."

Minutes later, we were treading our way towards the train station in a town masked with dust. Shades of earth tones had overtaken everything in sight—the men's clothing, the cars, the shops, even the store signs, which might have once displayed lively colors.

A white-pillared building stood out against the tan landscape, reminding me of a minuscule and plain version of the Roman buildings in the *Asterix & Obelix* comic strips. We merged with a large crowd of other passengers under the station's high ceiling. Joubin and I struggled to push through the bodies of other harried passengers while our parents' firm grasp directed us towards the guard. Then, over the hissing sound of the steam engine and the raised voices of travelers and conductors, I overheard bits and pieces of conversations among Nasser, Hamid, and my father, like "checking passports," "better trained," and so on, before we stopped near the passport control. I didn't pay too close a mind until I seized upon the words "the women's section of the train."

No one had mentioned anything about men's and women's sections, I thought angrily. I did not want to sit separated from my father and Joubin. I didn't want to be away from Hamid or Nasser either, for that matter. But my thoughts had no place there and then; my silent apprehensions and fears would have to follow me as we inched our way forward behind Nasser and then Hamid, who was holding all our tickets and his own passport in his hand. I recognized that we had come to the moment they had discussed in our hotel room. Hamid reached the guard, who was not only trying to make sense of our pile of tickets but had to simultaneously keep control of anyone that might sneak past him.

Seconds, disguised as forever, clicked by as our fates were being determined by the man, who wore a sweater with a badge and matching beret. What I wouldn't give for Getafix's magic potion, I thought. We wouldn't even need to take a train. I'd carry everyone and run to Lahore.

But it was Hamid's impatient Urdu words and grim face that acted like a spell in the midst of the guard's shouts at a man who was standing alongside. Whatever Hamid said, I assumed, had to do with the crowds he was pointing to angrily as they pushed and shoved against us.

The guard handed back the passports to Hamid, never having opened the pages. He continued to shout at the crowd, as he waved us past him onto the platform. Hamid didn't look back at my parents. He kept walking until he put enough distance between us and the guard.

Amid the discreet and silent eye contacts between Javeed Agha and our group, Joubin's and my gazes were fixed on the vast green locomotive train that stood before us, awaiting our ascent.

"There'll be stops where we can come and see you," my father said to my mother under his breath. Then, following a light nod from Hamid, he added hurriedly, "Quickly! Follow them."

That was when time cheated me again as it changed its form, pulling my mother and me towards the locomotive. My body followed hers as we merged within the small crowd pushing to climb on the train. We could see the back of Maheen Khanum and her family, and forced our way closer to them, making our way through the compartments. From the window, I caught my father nodding to me. Only Joubin stood next to him—which meant I was *on* that train, forcing me to catch up with the moment, illusion or not.

Joubin looked so little next to him, his eyes following our every movement, his little hands holding on to our father's, as mine were on my mother's and we pushed our way past women holding crying children, chickens, and large bundles.

Train in the Snow didn't have any chickens on the train, I said to myself—of that I was sure. What if something happened? I continued to follow Maheen Khanum's family, heading to a wooden bench that was solely occupied by a woman in her fifties. Anyone from our group who spoke Urdu would be in the men's section, I said mutely as Javeed Agha stepped onto the bench to place Layla's bag on the upper compartment, which was also to function as a sleeper.

The sudden outcry from our benchmate distracted me from my internal voices. Her complaints had begun when Javeed Agha rearranged some of the bags above. What was she upset about? Javeed Agha waved his arms and pointed to the bags and luggage on both sleepers, which ended in stern Urdu words that seemed to revolve around her oversized, rolled pile that covered the entire leg space between the benches.

"Here," he told us, pointing to the benches, a strand of frustration still lingering in his voice. "It's the only free space that seats you all together. You're gonna have to make do with this stack in front of you. She says she's carrying fragile things in there, so she doesn't want anyone placing their feet or legs on them."

"What exactly should we do with our legs?" Layla's mother

barked. Layla smiled, but no one else did. I crawled onto the hard bench and sat beside our new travel mate, whose teal shawl covered most of her short, round body.

I knew my tailbone would scream if I were to rest my weight on it again. This stretch of our trip would have to be made sitting on my side, I thought, pulling my legs in beneath me, this time leaning on my mother's shoulder. Layla's crawl toward the window on the adjacent bench amused me, maybe because she always seemed to just make do with whatever came her way, or maybe it was that she was followed by her mother's grunts, a clear protest against the gray pile that had stolen our leg space.

"I'll have to get off now," Javeed Agha said in a rush. "We'll check in on you whenever there's a long stop."

After nodding to him, none of us said much. We watched the busy settling of other women, who all seemed to have four things in common: one or two nose studs, wrists covered with yellow gold bangles, children in arms, and plenty of bundles in hand. The dull green pastel walls of the train, which seemed to have been bearing its stains and smudges for a long time, didn't contribute to our spirits. Not until we saw four women spreading their blankets on the soiled ground, to create a place to sit, did we realize how fortunate we had been to be sitting on the hard wooden benches.

"How do we know where Dad and Joubin are?" I asked my mother.

"They're at the back of the train," she answered reassuringly.

Finally, we felt ourselves drift out of the station. Shortly after, we were surrounded by the now-familiar backdrop of the dusty land, tan earth, and distant gray hills. I was more interested in our bench mate, who was wearing tiny toothpicks as nose studs. She seemed as intrigued about us as I about her. The other women on the train shared her curiosity. How can they tell we're not from here? I wondered. We're only a couple of shades lighter. But couldn't we pass for Pakistanis from the North? Maybe they don't have North and South shades, as we do in Iran. Maybe it's because we're not wearing nose studs or bangles. We might as well have stayed in our airplane clothes and not bothered trying to blend in.

"Is it time for lunch yet, you think?" asked Maheen Khanum after some time.

"Yes, it's one o'clock. Let's eat," my mother answered. "It'll give us something to do."

Layla had grabbed her bag to reach for the eggs when her mother noticed a young woman trying to pass through the crowd of women seated on the ground.

"That baby can't be more than a week," said Maheen Khanum.

"What baby?" Layla asked, looking up from her bag.

"So tiny," her mother said, as she pointed to the little bundle in the thin woman's arms. "Traveling with a newborn under these conditions."

"Well, at least the baby is with her mother," I said, and immediately Maheen Khanum's gaze was upon me. I was bursting to wipe away her frown and tell her about our friend Iran Khanum, but quickly caught my words before they got away from me, stuffing them back into my stomach, where they had been simmering. I had briefly forgotten that it was still not safe to tell. What if they believed in the stories too, the same stories that Iran Khanum had been compelled to sit through in her classroom as a little girl. At home she'd been taught to love all faiths and their Messengers, at school that Bahá'ís turned out the lights at their gatherings so men and women could feel one another in the dark, and the Islamic Republic labeled her community "enemies of Islam." One day after school, she had run home sobbing to her mother—a force who wasn't scared of the teacher, the town, or the fruit seller. "My money has the same picture of the Shah as yours. Why isn't it good enough to buy your fruits?" she had argued in that small town in Fazel Abad. Eventually, not even the corner store would sell her flour, so she could bake her own bread.

My mother's silent stare had reminded me not to speak about Iran Khanum's arrest as an adult in Tehran, five nights after the birth of her baby girl. The Pasdaran had pounded down their doors in the middle of the night, shouted her arrest and her husband's, forcing them to leave behind their newborn and their screaming two-year-old son with their aunt. At Evin prison, she had wept and begged to be returned to her nursing infant, holding her inflamed breasts.

"How dare you bear the name of our country!" she'd heard a woman shout at her while she was blindfolded, feeling the muzzle of a rifle against her spine. But after two days, her release had been announced. "What about my husband?" she had asked.

"He's gone," a Pasdar had said.

"Gone where?"

"Gone! *Dead!*"

She had been driven four streets away from the prison and let go. When she untied the black strap from her eyes, she'd found herself standing in the middle of a snow-covered street in a foreign neighborhood: still in her nightgown, with no coat, no money, no husband, and no sucking baby to relieve the shooting pain in her solid breasts, which had doubled in size. She had finally guessed her way home to her children.

Two days later, her husband had appeared at her door, too.

SUDDENLY, OUR MATE'S JARRING voice shot towards Layla. When she saw our blank faces, she pointed to Layla's foot. Her toes were touching the gray bundle. Realizing that she had crossed the frontier, she quickly pulled her foot away.

"What nerve," muttered Layla's mother under her breath.

"I wonder what she's carrying that can't take the pressure of a couple of toes," my mother added.

Layla just smiled. I didn't. I was angry. I didn't know why I was so angry. It had been her toes, after all, that crossed the line that was not to be crossed, and *she* had been the recipient of this woman's scolding. And though Layla had obviously shrugged it off, I somehow couldn't help but sit in my pot of anger stew, eating my hard-boiled eggs.

Perhaps sending food to my stomach contributed to the fading of my anger towards the Watch-Woman, who had also taken out her own eggs to eat.

"So what do you think is in this thing?" asked Maheen Khanum.

"A television," I guessed.

"A magnificent crystal chandelier," said Layla mockingly.

"Yeah." Her mother nodded sarcastically. "That would be my guess, too!"

"Do you want to take a nap?" my mother asked me after lunch.

Why not? I thought as I laid my head on my mother's lap. I couldn't sleep, but it felt nice to lie on my mother's thighs, careful not to have my curled legs touch our bench mate or her gray territory. Yet somehow, over the span of the following hour, my knee invaded the border. We didn't need to speak her language to understand what the Watch-Woman was telling my mother in complaint, nor did I have to wait for my mother to react. My knees withdrew.

What was the thick wool blanket concealing? I wanted to know more than ever. What had turned this woman into a dragon guarding its castle? Maybe it was a person, I thought. No, that's crazy. Well, not so crazy, but highly unlikely. Then what? I looked at the hennaed fingers resting on her thighs and slowly drifted to my waking dreams, to my *roya*. It's what my real name meant after all. Roya. Waking dreams. Vision.

Visions of finding friends I had lost after they left Iran, reuniting with my teacher, perhaps even seeing our friends from the Austria years, especially my first friend, met in a crib at six months of age. It didn't matter that I had had no way of knowing where to look for any of them. I had found them in my name.

"Is this a stop?" wondered Maheen Khanum in mid-afternoon.

"Doesn't look like there's anything here," said Layla.

"I think they've stopped to pump water into the reserve," my mother said after seeing a lonesome water pump by the tracks. "There are some other people at the pump. I'll be right back. Just want to rinse my hands."

"Go," nodded Maheen Khanum. "I'll be here."

In keeping with my mother's hygiene instructions, I kept a two-inch distance from the grimy window to look at the small crowd lined up behind the pump. My heart lifted when I saw Javeed Agha standing at the water pump as well. It had to mean that my father and Joubin were close by. I scanned the entire grounds but only saw other people's fathers and brothers.

Joubin must be asleep—that's why they can't leave the train, I said to myself, seeing that my mother's turn at the water pump was coming up.

How lonely, I thought when I saw the man who seemed to be the pump attendant return to the small, shabby cabin that stood nearby the rails. What does he do out here in the middle of nowhere with nothing but dry earth? I was wondering when I felt myself glide slowly by. The train was leaving. Where was my mother?

I quickly glanced back at the water pump. She was still on the ground.

"*Mommy!*" I shouted through the opening of my window. Maheen Khanum and Layla rushed to my side. "*Ya Khoda! Ya Khoda!*" screamed Maheen Khanum when she saw my mother running toward the train. But we had picked up speed and she was no longer visible. In my terror, I stared at Maheen Khanum, only I couldn't really see her through my tears. I was waiting for her to shout that she was onboard.

"Ah!" was all that came out of her mouth as she ran towards the door, Layla and I fast by her tail. Before we reached the door, however, it flung open and my mother appeared through it.

"Oh!" gasped Maheen Khanum out of breath.

I threw myself into my mother's arms, unaware of how we made it back to our wooden seats, back to our bench mate, who steadily guarded her territory.

It took some time before my internal poundings eased back to a regular rhythm.

"Where's your shoe?" asked Layla, when my mother lifted her legs onto the bench.

"It fell on the tracks when I jumped on the step."

My mother took off her remaining black shoe with the tan-striped heel and peered down at it awhile. I could almost hear her thoughts. They had been her only shoes. Now, somewhere by the tracks, in the middle of a lonely and forgotten land, lay a woman's shoe with a small label that read Made in Italy.

"Wait, I have a pair," said Layla. From her bag, she pulled out cloth slippers that must once have been white.

"Thank you, Layla," said my mother.

"Don't know if they'll fit."

"They will."

They didn't.

"Maybe if you keep the back heel down," suggested Maheen Khanum.

"Don't want to ruin them."

"You see how old they are. You can keep them. Don't know why I even brought them," said Layla, then paused. "Well, I guess now I know why I brought them."

"I don't know what I would've done in the middle of no-man's land," said my mother in a trembling voice. "No language, no money, no ID, no train 'til the next day. . . ."

"You *made* it!" said Maheen Khanum, who for the first time used a tone that told us that all was okay.

Yet I couldn't let go of the image of my mother running towards the train, or of the possible scenario she had just painted. What would we have done? How would we have found my father to tell him? The hows and whats were making my chest feel heavy.

The single seat beside us was empty.

"Can I sit there for a bit?" I asked my mother and climbed over her after receiving her approval.

The warm breeze that brushed against my face through the open window washed away the nightmarish possibilities. The distant mountains and the arid scenery hadn't changed much from the time we had left Zahedan. I missed the landscape of Tehran, the green trees, snow-topped Mount Damavand, visible from most parts of the city. Had it not been for some of the colorful clothing on the village women and children we occasionally passed, there would have been few signs of life, just more and more of the same dry and infertile country.

None of us dared to descend at the next station for any reason. I didn't even know what time it was anymore. I had stopped asking. It only lengthened our trip tenfold. It seemed to be close to sunset; that was enough to know. The bustle of passengers below my window amplified my yearning to have our journey end as well. Yet it all became bearable again when I saw my father approaching our window. I hadn't even noticed the food and blanket he was carrying until he handed them to us through the open window.

"Hurry back to your wagon," my mother said to him.

"Where's Joubin?" I asked.

"Nasser's looking after him on the train," he answered.

I wanted to ask whether he was sleeping, but my mother nervously interjected, "The train might leave. We're fine. Go back. Hurry!"

After he disappeared, my mother held out the tip of the *naan* that was peeking out from the brown paper bag my father had given her. As we each broke off a piece, our Watch-Woman dove into her bag, too. She took out her own piece of *naan* before it was too late to partake in the feast.

Dusk was moving in, and I welcomed it, tired of daylight and all it revealed.

JAVEED AGHA'S VISIT TO us the following hour was swift, mostly due to Maheen Khanum's insistence.

"Go before the train leaves you behind like it almost did Khandan Khanum."

"At the pump?" he asked in surprise.

"Yes," she nodded. "Now *go!*"

Where had this man come from? I wondered when I turned

my attention back from the window and saw a tall figure in an old dusty navy suit standing by our side, causing the Watch-Woman to become more animated. Too young to be her husband and too old to be her son; perhaps a brother? I thought. Whoever he was, she had a lot to say to him. An occasional word or sound was all he offered in return.

The big moment came when he indicated through gestures that our Watch-Woman intended to stretch out on the bench and that my mother and I would need to sleep above.

My mother and Maheen Khanum didn't need Urdu words to tell him that these barren regions would first have to become luscious and green before any of us would move up to the sleeper. If anyone was moving above, it would have to be her. His plan didn't have a glimmer of hope. The stern faces of the duo, underscored by their firm Farsi "no" and "up" were potent enough. To have it backed by angry fingers pointing at the enormous bundle and the above sleeper removed any space for negotiation.

Then it happened!

He not only crossed the barrier, but he applied two hundred pounds of his weight onto it. We stared at his large black shoes, supporting him on the top center of the gray bundle, the great fort. The four of us sat back without a sound, wide eyed, looking at him like a school of cod. He balanced himself on the bundle and moved one bag from one sleeper to the adjacent one, leaving a few to serve as pillows. A million questions flooded my mind from every direction. Why had she made us so uncomfortable? What was she protecting? How is her short, plump body going to get up there?

This man is a giant!

Then my questions froze when we saw what came next. She, our very own bench mate and Watch-Woman, did the unforgivable.

She stepped on the treasured pile, too.

They were *both* standing on it!

She hoisted a foot onto her brother's cupped palms and lifted herself up towards the sleeper. It was as if we were in a movie theatre, fully absorbed in every second. Would she fit? Would she fall?

I watched her struggle and felt sorry for her. I couldn't understand why she had turned our long hours together into a live version of Operation, the board game I used to have back home— only in this version, we weren't trying to remove any valuable organs or body parts yet still received the alarming buzzes.

Somehow, it didn't seem to matter much anymore. I hoped she wouldn't fall.

Her brother finally left, once she was safely resting above. It felt strange to sit there without her strange but peaceful. The sense of liberation from her didn't hit me until I saw Maheen Khanum extend her legs onto the gray pile.

"Stretch out your legs, Layla," she ordered. Her daughter hesitantly complied, as if uncertain of this newfound freedom. My mother was not uncertain. She quickly straightened her legs, leaned back, and directed me to lie on the bench, using her lap as my pillow. Darkness had filled the cabin, which finally allowed me to sink into sleep on the vibrating bench with no further thought of our Watch-Woman.

THE STOP AT A station the next morning woke most of us from our sleep. My mother noticed that one of our blankets was missing. It took us a few minutes to discover that it had been used by a couple of women to sleep on the ground, for which we had no words of complaint.

The man in the navy suit reappeared to retrieve his sister from the above sleeper. Again we watched as our bench mate hauled her way down. The moment she was safely on the bench, her familiar outcry shot across to our legs that rested on her bundle.

"Enough!" Maheen Khanum shouted back in Farsi.

"No!" my mother said in support, leaning in over me to point her index finger at our Watch-Woman, who stared back in surprise. Neither let go of her gaze for what seemed like a very long time. I had played that stare game with my cousin countless times.

My mom won.

We had all won. From that point on, we stretched out our legs on top of the bundle, grateful for the difference it made to our bodies and spirits.

We ate bread, and so did our retired Watch-Woman.

"I need to go to the bathroom," I told my mother close to midday.

"I think it's at the end," said Maheen Khanum.

We climbed over knees and feet along the narrow aisle to move forward. We didn't need language to find directions, as we were guided by the odor. I instantly regretted my call for a bathroom adventure, especially since it wasn't urgent. I couldn't imagine how it was going to pan out. In the best of hotels, we had to wait until the toilet was covered with my mother's protective methods against germs. The foul smell was making me nervous. My mother opened the door and slammed it shut immediately, her entire body twitching in disgust. *"Ahh!"*

Our two-second glimpse of a floor covered with feces had us both hurrying back to our seats with grimaced faces.

"What happened to you?" asked Maheen Khanum when we returned to our bench.

My mother's shaking head had to serve as an answer until a later time. One thing became clear: I would have to hold it. It proved not to be as difficult as we thought, since we weren't consuming any water or anything else other than bread and eggs.

Just when my mother and I had distracted ourselves enough from the horrid scene in the restroom, we saw Layla's pained face.

"What?" asked my mother turning to Layla's fixed gaze.

"Oh," sighed my mother after seeing a young woman carrying her diarrhea-covered baby in mid-air, a foot away from her own soiled clothes.

"She won't be able to do much in that bathroom," said my mother, her face in her palm, as the woman passed down the corridor.

"It's that bad?" asked Maheen Khanum.

"Worse!"

When the young mother returned, she was holding her naked baby in one arm and the soiled cloth diaper in the other.

Feeling something between repulsed and impressed, I observed the mother's ingenious method of using speed and the outside air to create a dryer on a train by suspending most of the diaper outside and slamming the window onto one end of it, a technique adopted by other mothers on the train whose diapers were also covered in stains. For the next hour, my mind wandered back home as I blankly watched the diapers flapping against the wind.

"Again?" asked Maheen Khanum after some time, as we watched the reenactment of an earlier scene with the young woman and her diarrhea-covered baby.

"It's the other twin," I answered.

"Poor woman," said Maheen Khanum.

I felt sick, but not as sick as when I saw the mother of the twins take the suspended diaper from the window and wrap it around her baby, a scene my mother tried to escape by leaning her head back for a nap. I wanted to sleep too, but I knew that I wouldn't fall asleep. It would have to wait until nightfall.

I returned to my memories that played before me like a mirage.

Lucid, baby-blue waters caress my body as I swim deep to grab a rock I tossed to the bottom of the pool, seeing the shimmer of the beaming sun above, whiffing the scent of chlorine, tasting its salty flavor. I lie belly down on the warm blocks of stones surrounding the pool. Trickles of water tickling my back, I pick up a leaf of fresh grass and use it as a lifeboat for the insects that have been struggling in the waters, lining them up on the pavement as in a makeshift infantry hospital, waiting for their wings to dry so that they can fly back to their lives.

WHEN MY MOTHER PASSED out the sweets from the paper bag my father had given us the night before, we didn't think that it would set our bench mate into a distraught frenzy, combing through her belongings to find something comparable to eat. She found none, leaving her no choice but to point to the dry pastries we were eating.

"You got to be kidding me," mumbled Maheen Khanum but didn't protest when my mother handed the woman one of our sweets. So we sat, treating ourselves, and for the first time we saw our ex-Watch-Woman smile. I smiled back.

I moved to the empty single seat by the adjacent window again and watched the goat and the two chickens that had just left our train. So had the twins, their mother, and their bundles. That must be the twins' dad, I thought when I saw a man on the platform carrying one of the babies, moving quickly ahead of the other two members of his family. I wanted to leave the train as well, to feel the soil under my feet. I'd had enough of the tracks and the shakiness; tired of the smell, the wooden benches, and the separation from my father and Joubin. I envied the people on the ground who were on their way to their families, as we rolled away from them in hope of completing a voyage that seemed to have no end.

Then, suddenly, the people on the ground began waving their arms, in their efforts to hail the train.

"Oh, no!" I exclaimed.

"What?" asked my mother, rushing toward my seat.

"We've left that man behind," I said in a panic.

Our train was following a curve in the tracks, which gave us a clear view of the man, in his light brown *shalvar khamis,* running with all his might. We left him running. My mother was holding her mouth and I wanted to burst into tears.

"What's gonna happen to him now?" I asked.

"He'll be okay. He'll catch the next train," she answered, but I knew she was only trying to console me.

"His stuff's on *this* train!"

"He must be traveling with friends. They'll look after his stuff."

He had become a tiny figure in the background, far away from the station, out in the middle of who knows where, with only the distant gray mountains to keep him company.

No one would believe any of this, I thought. Not about this place, or almost losing my mother at the train station, or leaving behind that poor man. No one would believe the guard with the machine gun, the other guard's tea break at the second border, the dry riverbed in the middle of nowhere, the hut with the missing roof, the Nivea cream saving our lives. . .none of it! *I* even found it hard to believe that, only three weeks before, Joubin and I had been playing with our kittens in our backyard. How was it that we were now riding through another land, in a train that was nothing like the one in *Train in the Snow*, on our way to be reunited with our relatives in Germany?

How did all this happen?

My prayers?

My prayers.

My grandmother's prayers.

For hours, we rode past the run-down huts and those who dwelled in them by the roadside, and I made promises and vows.

You have to tell this story. You have to remember everything. Can't forget any of this. See the young mother's yellow *shalvar khamis* with the little orange patterns on it. Don't forget the little naked boy standing next to his big sister by the road. Write about the donkeys with their lowered heads as they carry their heavy loads. Don't miss the women washing clothes in their flat plastic tubs. Note the cloth bundles that are carried by the young and old alike.

It will end soon. I will be free of Golbakht, the stranger; I'll be rid of the hiding and pretending, purged from the silence, free to trust.

My name is Roya. I am a Bahá'í, and I escaped from Iran.

"This is it. We're in Lahore," my mother said on our thirty-second hour on the train.

Chapter Four

Had the ground not been covered with spit marks, I would have stretched my entire body against its stillness. Yet neither the grunge nor our pace allowed for idling. It was enough just to have the soles of my feet feel the dusty ground as we searched through the crowd to find the rest of our group.

"I see them," said my mother looking into the distance. I couldn't see anything beyond the bodies moving, pushing, bumping past one another. The firm grip of my mother's hand, the hurried steps towards our male party, and the voices of the crowd made me feel that we were moving closer to the end—the end of running. We had reached Lahore, so Germany couldn't be much farther away in the plans.

Our mothers carefully steered us through the large group of

passengers who were also waiting to get off the platform. At last we merged with the others, strategically positioning ourselves behind Nasser and Hamid. Joubin and I caught a glimpse of each other. Any words between us would have been lost in the midst of the bodies between us.

Why do they need to check our tickets and identities when we're *leaving* the station? I thought, moments before the guard asked to see Nasser's passport. For a second, I didn't even care anymore, because I was losing my breath. I reached for air, using my elbows as my shield to push away the encroaching crowd. Nasser pointed to Joubin and me as he complained in Urdu, no doubt using Hamid's tactic to pull us out of the mass, impatient to exit. It worked.

By the time we had reached the street, Joubin was connected to our mother's hand, back to the order of things that had been established since we began our journey: men in front, women and children steps behind.

Really? I thought when I saw us approaching a restaurant.

Old faded posters hung from the smoky walls of the modest establishment. The aroma of spices was a welcomed change from the odors we had breathed in on the train. The stews, *naan*, and french fries that Nasser and Hamid helped carry to our table flirted with our senses.

"These are for the kids," Nasser said smiling, distributing the plates of the golden fried potato strips. Even though the stews were too spicy for us young ones, their mere scent was captivating. We were thrilled to dip our fries in ketchup. I smiled at Nasser, but he didn't see. The ordeal was behind us and Germany before us.

What I hadn't anticipated after dinner was that we would be saying goodbye to Layla's family outside the restaurant. Time was escaping again, robbing me of what I would have wanted to say to Layla—not in words, for it wasn't in them that I could express what I needed her to know. It hadn't occurred to me that they were not heading to Germany like us. Why had I thought that they'd continue that stretch of our journey with us? It felt unnatural to part ways.

They jumped into a white minibus, and we jumped into another one with Nasser and Hamid.

"Are we going to Germany now?" I said in a hushed voice to my mother in the minibus.

"Not yet," she told me. "It'll be a while still before we get there."

"Where're we going now?"

"To Rawalpindi," she said.

Where's that? I wondered, but I didn't ask. It made no difference, and I was too tired. We drove into the dark, through the busy streets, chiming in with the honking. Before long I was lost in sleep against my mother's arm.

It was past midnight when we arrived at our motel, which struggled to live up to its one and half stars yet far surpassed a truck, desert, or train in providing us a refuge and a couple of beds to collapse on.

"I'll go make the call," my father said.

"Who are you calling?" I asked him.

"Papaji," he answered.

"Can I come with you?"

"Sure, but you won't be able to talk to him, okay?"

I nodded. We walked down a narrow hallway overpowered by a strong smell of sandalwood and covered in stained burgundy carpets. Corner steps led us down to a little room. A glass fridge, a tiny table, and two chairs became our backdrop as my father stood by the telephone that hung on the wall. Some English words passed between my father and the attendant of the fridge, which I gathered had to do with the upcoming call.

"Is this the Pakzad residence?" my father shouted on the phone in Farsi.

Who is Pakzad? I wondered.

"Oh, forgive me. It's not the Pakzad's, then," he continued, smiling. "So sorry to wake you, sir."

Before I could formulate my next question, I heard him say: "That's the number I have, Operator."

"All right. Thank you," he said, then after a long pause repeated his request to speak to Mr. Pakzad.

"Don't worry, Operator. I must have written the number wrong. Let's not wake anyone else up tonight. Thank you!"

Click! Then a smile, and more dialing. This time he didn't ask for Mr. Pakzad. This time he said: "Mamanam, it's me."

Pari joon! It hadn't occurred to me that we could call out to America and speak to her.

"Yes, we're visiting Rawalpindi. The family says hello," he said beaming. "...Yes! How are you?" he asked, his voice lifting again. Is he talking to someone else now? I wondered.

"Wait one second," he said and waved to me. I took the receiver from him and found myself speaking to my aunt. The last time I had seen her was when she visited us in Tehran when I was six years old. I didn't remembered what she sounded like.

"I hope to see you very soon, Azizam!" she said to me. In my mumbled response, all I could hear and think of was her clear and untainted voice—a voice that danced freely in my head.

"Thank you!" he said to the attendant, who nodded himself back to sleep.

"But we didn't call Papaji yet!" I exclaimed, not wanting to move from my spot.

"We did."

"When?"

"Let's go upstairs. Will tell you in a minute."

I didn't need to ask any of my own questions, since my mother's were quite thorough and repetitive. For the second time, my father recounted the conversation he had had on the telephone.

"When I asked if it was the Pakzad residence, Papaji said, 'No, sir, it's not,'" mimicking my grandfather in a jolly voice. "So I apologized. And that's when the operator from Tehran came on the line and double-checked the number."

"He just came on the line?" asked my mother.

"Very quickly."

It was the first time that we had the monitored telephone lines in Iran so openly revealed to us.

"So the operator dialed the number himself and connected me to Papaji again," he continued. "When your father picked up, he happily told me that I had the wrong residence. The operator kept repeating, 'Apologies for waking you up again so late at night, Agha.'"

"What did Papaji say after that?" my mother asked, hanging on to my father's every word.

"'Oh, it's all right, Operator,' he kept saying," said my father, impersonating Papaji in a light, friendly voice. "'Don't worry about it.'"

My father's laughter helped my mother laugh too, which to me meant that we were closer to Germany.

What were my grandparents doing, now that they had received our call in the middle of the night? Were they sitting up in bed, going over every word, as we had? Was my grandmother crying? Would they be able to go back to sleep?

Our first contact with home after seven days: They'll probably be able to sleep better than on any of the other nights, I reasoned, thinking about what it must have felt like not knowing what had happened to us after we left their doorstep. Tired of the scenes in my head, I shifted all my attention to the luxury that awaited, our beds. Joubin had already been bathed and was fully asleep.

In the cracked shower, I washed away the two-day build up of sweat and odor residue from my pores and changed into my nightgown. Clean and exhausted, I climbed into bed next to Joubin, stretching my body, still hearing my aunt's graceful voice. I didn't care about the discoloration of the sheets or the musty smell of the blanket; it was a bed, I had a pillow under my head, and it was divine.

The drawn velvet curtains kept us in bed well past dawn. We woke to my mother pulling open the burgundy curtain to let sunlight fill the room. I was curious to see what her gaze was fixed on and remained puzzled after I took a peek, for there wasn't much to look at beyond the wall of a derelict building.

"Let's get some breakfast," my father said in a way that made me look forward to it. A knock on Hamid and Nasser's door initiated our foray into streets that seemed to have been there forever, and forgotten.

I followed my mother's footsteps but my attention was immersed in the bicycle that had been converted to a newsstand, the tables that supported stacks of black and brown flip-flops, the neglected buildings covered in signs, the advertising in characters I could read yet was unable to draw meaning from, the fruit attendant sitting in the center of his station, encircled by propped up boxes of neatly arranged fruits.

"What are those black spots on all the fruit?" my mother asked, approaching to gain a better view. They were flies—flies ready for breakfast. Despite them, my mother's face grew bright: *"Limu shirin!"*

"And bananas!" I added. "They have bananas here."

We hadn't had bananas for years. They had stopped selling them back home.

"Can we get clementines?" my brother asked, joining in the excitement. Clementines were another fruit we hadn't tasted in a while. "Oh, and grapes. How about grapes?"

"We'll stick to the fruits we can peel," she declared. She waved the unwanted pests aside to select the choicest fruits, and we strolled our way back to our hotel.

"They have a Bata here too," I said to her, pointing to a red-and-white sign across the street. I remembered buying my last pair of shoes from their store in Tehran.

Seeing Bata, and the bag of fruits, made up for the spit-infested grounds, the smaller muddy roads, and the standing water they contained.

In our room, I helped my mother wash the clementines, bananas, and *limu shirins*, because it made her feel better to peel clean fruit. Nasser entered our room with a tray of *doodh patti* to complement our breakfast. We feasted on the tastes of home, inhaled the perfumes that took me back to the afternoons spent with loved ones around large platters of fruit with little side plates. The aroma of *limu shirin* transported me to the rose bushes in my grandparents' yard, where my cousin Schabi and I had slurped our *limu shirins* between games, pretending to be Charlie's Angels. Everyone knew that the best way to enjoy the yellow fruits was to squeeze and suck the juice from the small hole we'd poke in one spot. We had skipped this delight in Rawalpindi, since we couldn't press our lips against the skin, yet we still relished the taste once my mother finished peeling them. I wished Layla was still with us. She would surely have liked to feast on the treasured fruits, I thought, but I guessed that she'd already discovered them wherever she was in Lahore.

We spent much of the morning in our room, removed from the dirty conditions, and from attention and suspicion. I didn't mind. It was easier being Golbakht away from the curious eyes.

We shared our tales about our journey on the green locomotive, my mother's sprint towards our moving train, her lost shoe,
my brother's makeshift bed, the goats, the chickens, and the man
who was left behind.

"What do you think happened to him?" I asked. "And his
stuff?"

"Oh, I'm sure he found his way to wherever he was going,"
Nasser said with soft eyes. "His friends looked after his things
until they met up with him again."

I nodded, seemingly satisfied. I didn't believe his story, but I
appreciated it nonetheless.

By noon, we were back in a white minibus heading to Islamabad for the day, this time traveling with a couple of other passengers.

"Women and children in the back, men in front," Nasser had
decreed before we ascended.

"My apologies, but are you Iranians?" asked one of the male
passengers in Farsi.

"Yes," replied Hamid dryly; he was obviously going to be leading the conversation.

"Good to meet you," the man replied with a nod, placing his
hand on his chest as usually done in Iran to show respect.

Is this good or bad? I wondered, trying to ascertain our situation with this stranger from Iran.

"I'm here from America, trying to find out what I can do for my brother. They arrested him in Karachi for finding him without a visa. They just stopped him in the middle of the street and asked for his passport," he said, shaking his head.

"Who?" Hamid asked.

"The police. He was leaving his motel, and they were waiting for him across the street. It was probably someone from the motel staff. The authorities have tons of spies looking out for Iranian escapees."

Dead silence followed for a few minutes before the stranger added, "Forgive my intrusion—I don't want to pry—but should you be in the same situation as my brother was, I would highly advise you to seek protection from the UN Refugee Commission in Islamabad."

When Hamid redirected the conversation back to his brother, I leaned over to my mother to whisper, "Why are we going to Islamabad?"

"We're trying to find a way to get to Germany from there, but first we want to see what it's like."

Trying? Find a way?

"Can't we just fly to Germany?" I whispered, worrying about her answer.

"We need to get a visa. We'll have to see how long it will take from Islamabad." Her words made Germany seem even farther out of reach. I didn't know much about the process of attaining visas in Pakistan; any references I had stemmed from conversations I'd heard over time, and I remembered visas as scarce luxuries.

"May you be successful in helping your brother," "Thank you,"

"May my life be a sacrifice to you," "May God protect you," and such were exchanged between the men as we descended the bus. These are common expressions in Farsi. Iranians offer an abundance of praise, as well as their lives, to one another countless times on a daily basis—an encoded form of speech, culture, and expression. Of course, most don't mean it literally. It's the tradition of *taarof*. There are two rules to it. Under the first, you offer a pre-agreed understanding that you are not to be taken up on. The second rule mostly applies to food: you offer, the person refuses; you insist, they refuse; you insist again, maybe adding a bit of begging and pleading, which usually paves the way for the final acceptance. Still, it's tricky, much as Papaji once experienced even after years of living in Iran. Born to a Turkish mother, an Iranian father, and raised in Istanbul, Turkey, he always struggled with Iranian *taarof*.

Angry and flustered, he had come home one day after seeing the same *Haj Agha* on the corner of the street he passed often, the one who always invited him in for tea. That day, my grandfather had accepted, only to be told by an embarrassed *Haj Agha* that his wife was actually not home and he wouldn't be able to host him properly.

"Why offer in the first place?" Papaji had complained when he returned home, his hands flying in the air. "I didn't particularly *want* tea at that hour, but he always keeps insisting, 'Come, please, it would make me so happy,'" he'd gone on, mimicking the man in a piping voice.

I must have inherited some of that Turkish blood, since I

never mastered the art of knowing when to accept, refuse, insist, or give up in the intricate web of *taarofing*.

WHEN WE LEFT THE UN building a couple of hours later, thanks to the advice from the stranger on the bus, I was piecing together the gist of the English conversation my parents had had with the staff.

"I don't get it!" Hamid said, holding his forehead. "Why did you refuse refugee status? They would've given you money, too!"

"We don't need that status. And we have enough to get by," answered my father.

"'Til when?" Hamid asked, then lowered his voice. "That stack of gold isn't going to get you far. You don't know *how* long it will take to get a visa."

"Look, there're enough people who are in worse situations than we are. They'll need that money more than we do right now. We got what we needed. They'll issue us protection as long as we're on Pakistani soil. We just need to get proof that we're Bahá'ís."

"I don't understand you," Hamid said, shaking his head, as we walked.

"Right now, I have to figure out how to get word to my cousin in Austria to send us a letter that confirms we're Bahá'ís."

By the time we had reached our hotel back in Rawalpindi, it was dark. We spent some time in the small lobby, watching a cricket game on television with Nasser and Hamid, while, in the next room, my parents tried to call my father's cousin. Even with the television on, I could hear his voice projecting into Austria. His coded words reminded me that walls still had ears.

THE NEXT MORNING, WE bought more fruit and, this time, cucumbers from the same fruit seller. If he only knew that his fruits were the highlight of my days spent in Rawalpindi—that they allowed the scent of home to overpower the murmur of plans to leave for Islamabad. I wasn't interested in the details—the only one that concerned me was to know when we would leave for Germany, for which no one had an answer I liked, wanted, or needed.

As my mother peeled the cucumbers in our room, my mind drifted to my friend Omid, who, like me, was ten years old and who was still in Tehran. I thought about our hide-and-seek games at his grandparents' home. I thought about the scent of cucumbers that had perfumed their living room during one of our many visits surrounded by tea and fruit. I remembered his father helping me to dress my small teddy bear, as if it was his very own cub.

I wished that we had said goodbye to him. Of course, during my thoughts, and my regrets over leaving them behind, I didn't know that they were going to arrest and execute Omid's father years later, or that his grandfather would be found in the middle of the street with a fatal wound to the back of his head, and I never dreamed that my playmate, Omid, would, years later, be sitting in solitary confinement, awaiting charges, any charges, that would determine his crime and fate. All I knew then was that Omid was on the other side of the border, and that we were supposed to be free on this one.

"We'll leave at dusk," Hamid said.

Leave to go where? What had I missed? I waited until he and Nasser left our room before asking my parents.

"To Islamabad," my father explained. "We're going to stay there for a while, until we get our visas for Germany."

"Will it take long?" I asked, not knowing why I'd even asked; I knew there was no way for him to know that.

"Let's go and see," he said lightly, always striving to see the sky blue.

I looked at my mother. She was quiet, but her dark eyes weren't.

That afternoon, on our walk to buy some *naan*, my mother suddenly burst into laughter. She covered her mouth, her laughter preventing her words from trickling out, and began to say, "Commer. . ." before a roar of laughter swallowed the rest of the word. Whatever it was, it instantly had me joining in. Joubin and the men stopped in their tracks, staring, half smiling, half in confusion.

"*Commercial!*" she finally managed to say. "All this time, I was confused and shocked by these signs I was reading. They're English words written in Urdu characters! Commercial, not *Kamar Shol*. That other sign must mean 'Emergency,' then," she said, pointing to a yellow-and-red sign, I read as *Amreh Jensi*, hardly words that would be advertised so openly. Nasser held his stomach and laughed freely. Hamid and my father chuckled along as we continued our search for *naan*.

We spent the remaining hours, in our room before we left Rawalpindi for our next destination—Islamabad.

CHAPTER FIVE

THERE WERE NO WORDS uttered in our introduction to our motel room in Islamabad, only my mother's hand pointing towards the hole in the wall.

"Fix, fix," said the tired attendant, nodding to one side with assurance.

I counted eight stars through the missing bricks, wide enough to climb into the night.

Before my father returned from settling our paperwork at the front desk, my mother had made the attendant bring in new sheets, twice. After which, she resigned herself to sleeping in semi-clean sheets with holes close to the size of the one in our wall—a triumph nonetheless from the previous sets with yellow stains.

By then, we had become accustomed to having a room with a

drain in the center of our bathroom, a squat toilet in one of its corners, and a pipe sticking out of the wall serving as our shower.

"Oh, this one has a mirror," I said, looking above the sink.

My mother peeked in. "Well, that's good," she said softly.

"SHALL WE GO KNOCK on Hamid and Nasser's doors?" I asked the next morning.

"They're not staying here," my father explained. "Nasser and Hamid live in Islamabad. They have their own homes here."

"Here?" I asked, letting go of my half-made ponytail. "They were out, and they went back *into* Iran?"

"They study here," my father replied. "Sometimes they go back to help people escape. . . . Let's finish getting ready. They'll be here in a few minutes to show us around."

I grabbed those few minutes to mull what he had just told me.

When we saw Hamid and Nasser leave their taxi, I wanted to run to them. Instead, I smiled hello, hearing my own echos of thanks floating through my head.

Our arrival in Islamabad had marked the end of my life as Golbakht. I was released from the Baluch girl from Afghanistan, whose dialect I had never known but who had saved my life.

And though I earned my own name back, it was to belong to a different Roya. This one was to have no memories of escaping Iran; she was to be a mere tourist visiting Islamabad from Germany. There was one thing, however, that she shared in common with Golbakht: to share no secrets with the extra ears that might be lurking about.

And when the questions came, I gave no answers, as the mother of an Iranian family that spent three days at the same motel noticed. On the third night, while Joubin and I played with her two sons in the garden, she told my mother, "Whatever I ask your daughter, she says, 'I don't know.'"

"Good," said my father when my mother recounted that story to us later in our room. "It's best to dodge the questions with 'I don't know.'" And that's what we did. We dodged the spit marks covering the ground, ignored people's glances, avoided the motel owner's attempts to befriend us, and evaded the questions of an Afghan guest who stayed there for weeks. I didn't find it difficult to say, "I don't know," to him, since I struggled to understand his accent and expressions in a language we shared. My mother was better skilled at maneuvering through his inquiries, occasionally escaping his questions by joining Joubin and me in mid-play of *estop rangui* in the backyard, laughing at Joubin's race to nowhere screaming, "I don't know what color 'ultramarine' is."

The backyard of the motel was generous to us, lending its green grass for us to run on, offering its three small trees as our "home base," yielding its bushes for our games of Hide-and-Go-Seek. For my mother, it provided time to hear our laughter, our screams:

"You're it!"

"Safe!"

"*Mommy.*"

In her silence, she lined our wet clothes on a worn pink rope suspended between two pipes on the peeling cement walls. And,

during the wait for them to dry, she'd immerse herself in her English copy of a palm-reading book she'd bought from the bookstore
next to where she had also bought her sandals, her heels at last rid
of Layla's folded-in slippers. I felt slightly freer on the days that
my *shalvar khamis* was dripping dry because it meant that I was wearing my airport clothes, familiar and better themed for our personas
as visitors from Germany. Yet bearing only two changes of clothing
meant we were also still tied to the *shalvar khamis* we had worn as
Baluch Afghans, scrubbed and rescrubbed by our mother to their
original colors. Though we blended in slightly better with our long
tops and loose pants, it didn't shake the feeling of being a stranger
in a land I had briefly learned about in Geography class. Never
did I dream back then, that I would one day walk among its people
as an impostor.

"Sir, sir!" the motel owner, who was running towards my father,
called out after we had waved goodbye to our Iranian playmates
who were leaving the place, bringing to an end our shared three
nights of games and giggles. "A telephone call for you, sir." My father ran inside, with my mother, Joubin, and I trailing fast behind
him.

"Sheida jan!" he called out into the receiver. "How are you?"

"Khaleh?" I asked, wide-eyed, turning to my mother, who
quickly nodded.

"I called her a couple of nights ago," she whispered in a rush,
not wanting to miss what her sister might be saying.

"Yes, if you could check whether there's a market for saffron,
please," my father said, his voice taking over the entire hall. "We

can't talk much," he added in a quick whisper. "And *pistachios, too,* please. . . . Yes, *saffron and pistachios,*" he screamed, and again in a whisper added, "Not safe to talk often. . . . Great, if you could find a *market* there, that would be great!" he concluded loudly. ". . .Yes, yes, she's right here. . . . We must keep it brief," he mumbled to my mother as he passed the receiver to her.

"Yes, yes, all is well. We're seeing the city and hope to be back with you soon," my mother said brightly before she allotted the kisses she was sending to her sister's family.

"What's wrong?" I asked Joubin while she was saying her good-byes. Looking ill, he shrugged, bit his cheek, and leaned against our mother.

When she asked the same question after she had hung up with Germany, he said, "My throat hurts."

Ugh! I thought. Now she's going to make him gargle with salt water.

"Ah," said my mother instead, caressing his back. "You know, there'll be more kids here to play with, I'm sure. Guess where we're going today?"

Joubin shrugged.

"Nasser and Hamid want to take us to a restaurant for lunch," she said, smiling.

How do mothers know when we must gargle with salt water and when we just need some happy news? I wondered.

"WE'LL ASK 'EM NOT to make your food spicy," Nasser said, winking to us when he opened the door to a restaurant called Ali

Baba that had white tablecloths, black chairs, white-shirted wait-
ers—and a sound system.

"Bee Gees!" I cried out. Home. My father's face beamed as
well. It was he, after all, who owned their records and danced to
their music like John Travolta.

"Can we eat here every day?" I asked, holding on to his arm.

"We'll try to come here often," he answered, and I knew that
he was holding back from shaking his shoulders and elbows to "Ah-
Ah-Ah-Ah."

I drifted in the footsteps of our waiter, who was showing us to
our table. While Nasser ordered our meal to "How Deep is Your
Love," I was traveling back to our summer road trips to the slopes
of the Alborz mountain range, listening to the Gibb brothers along
the way, hiking with our dog Rexy, discovering hidden field flowers
between the rocks, washing our hands in the icy stream that traveled down from the snowy peak. On one of those trips, we had
come home earlier than planned. First to enter our house, I had
bounced past my parents' bedroom before freezing to a halt.

"Mommy! Daddy!" I screamed.

Within seconds, they had bolted to my side, and we had all
gaped at their bedroom bestrewn with papers, books, clothes, and
makeup, the contents of their dresser drawers tossed carelessly
about.

"A raid!" I'd said, immediately feeling fortunate to have been
in the mountains that day.

"I don't think so," my father had muttered, turning to the hallway. His suits rested in a neat pile on the carpet, his polished shoes

and belts arranged in a row beside them.

My parents had suddenly darted through every room in the house, Joubin and I bounding behind them in a panic.

"The balcony door is open, Bahman," my mother had shouted from our room.

My father'd run outside and scanned the grounds from above.

"Shall we call it in?" she asked.

"You call. I'll hide my books," my father replied. I followed him to the garden, where there was a minute closet that contained pipes and tools. He carefully slipped several Bahá'í books, covered in plastic bags, into different nooks and crannies. Once he strategically repositioned the garden equipment, we ran back upstairs.

After my mother made the call to the authorities, she swept through her scattered belongings.

"They took the pearls Mamaji and Papaji gave me," she said, tears building. "And the other ones. . .everything." She brushed aside her leopard-print silk scarf and black purse to sink on her bed. "Almost everything," she said in a broken voice, discovering the white-gold ring that cradled a little diamond, a gift from my father when I was born. I wanted to rest my hand on her, on her fist that was wrapped tightly around her gift. Yet the pile of things that lay in between us made it difficult to draw close. Instead, I opened the door to the two Pasdaran who were standing at our doorstep.

After they had searched the grounds in vain, the bearded men in green, with rifles on their shoulders, made a list of all that had been stolen.

"You listen to music?" one of them asked.

"What?" my mother had asked impatiently, in the midst of listing what she had lost.

"The stereo is on," he'd said, pointing to it with a nod.

"The kids were listening to their mermaid story!" my mother had said firmly, making her annoyance no secret.

"Careful Mommy," I'd whispered silently, remaining invisible.

WHEN I SAW OUR waiter with his full tray of steaming dishes, I felt as excited as I had when I won a ski race at Dizin one winter. Finally, a wholesome warm meal. Joubin and I had lived on *naan*, eggs, fruits, and cucumbers for seven days. I couldn't wait for my mother to finish spooning out the stews. I dipped a piece of *naan* in some sauce. At once, I flapped my hands about, looking as if I was ready to fly away. My impatience to start my meal had saved Joubin from a smoldering tongue. Nasser, who until then had been chuckling at Joubin and my "seated happy dance," was now on his feet, calling the waiter over in an angry voice. An exchange of Urdu between them quickly sent the waiter back to the kitchen.

"He'll make another dish for you," Nasser said to Joubin and me, his eyes as soft as his voice.

"He said that they didn't put chili peppers in it, just black pepper," Hamid explained calmly, with a suppressed smile. "Black pepper isn't spicy for them, it's flavorful."

While we waited for the chililess, pepperless food to arrive, swaying to "More than a Woman," I saw flashes of Travolta spinning his dance partner around their disco floor, remembering how

fortunate I had felt watching *Saturday Night Fever* at one of our visits
to my father's friends, wishing all the while that their films would
never get confiscated, that we would continue to be invited to
watch *Sleeping Beauty*, *Avalanche*, and videos of Googoosh.

"Oh, it's like *tahchin*," my mother said when the waiter had returned with the new dishes that showed mercy.

Ali Baba had brought us close to home. I fought my desire to
devour the yellow treasure on my plate. Time lingered on that occasion and repaid some of what it had stolen from us the last couple of weeks. Every spoonful was a balm, its steam warming my
face, its flavors reviving my body.

My father kept his word, and we dined at Ali Baba's as many
times we could, which amounted to once a week. Before entering,
I would anticipate the sudden switch to "Stayin' Alive" from the
local music that had played beforehand. It was a gift to us from
the owner—the moment we appeared through the doorway of the
cave that beheld great riches, where there was no need to empha-
size *mirch nahin, kali mirch nahin*. It was a place where my mother's
face was free of furrowed brows, her hands free of scrubbing
things, or us, with moist towelettes.

During our meals, my mind often wandered to Ali Baba and
the forty thieves, as well as to the other tales from *Shahrzad*, like Al-
addin and his oil lamp. I would have liked to own such a lamp, I
thought. But what if it was one of those lamps that only gave you
one wish? A type of question our Farsi teacher would have asked
us in our German school. I had always thought the life of a *djinni*
unfair, always about granting other people's wishes, turning slums

into palaces, yet always obliged to return to a life confined to a small lamp. In my self-created versions, I had made my wish to be the *djinni*'s release. But what would I do now? I thought, sitting at Ali Baba's. How would I use my one wish? Would I use it to free the *djinni*, or the people in Iran? Maybe once the *djinni* was freed, the taste of freedom would move it to free all those who weren't. But could I chance it?

Seeing that we couldn't always eat at Ali Baba's or the fish 'n' chips restaurant, which was the only other establishment that held back its hot spices for us, my parents bought a hot plate and an aluminum pot for our room. Though a lengthy road to soup, onion omelets, turnips, and the like, it made our meals a time to look forward to.

Naan, fruit, and tea set off our days, followed by our wait for the knock of one of the motel attendants expecting to clean our room. My mother would then have to say, "No, thank you, it's not needed," before we could leave for the day. It was a ritual we had taken up after my mother witnessed the motel's method of cleaning that first morning after our arrival.

The attendant had used a broom made of loose branches to clean the squat-toilet and then continued to scrub the rest of the bathroom floor with the same broom. My mother's gasps and cries had made me feel sorry for both her and the attendant. Her *akh*'s, *ah*'s, and *no*'s had driven the panic-stricken attendant to fetch some disinfectants. My mother had then proceeded to take on scrubbing the entire room on her hands and knees with Dettol. The antiseptic scent, which made my lungs burn and sinuses clear, had nonetheless been soothing, for it reminded me of the freshly mopped floors of the little corner stores back home.

Our most common outing came to be our trips to the embassies, one day the Canadian, another the Austrian, German, American, all saying what we didn't want to hear. Did they know that We Will Contact You, to us, meant that we couldn't venture too far from the motel in case there was a phone call? Or that It May Take Three To Six Months meant an eternity to someone like my mother?

The wait for the calls that never came pushed us into the streets, wandering about, stopping at the shops, overpowered by the sweet and spicy scents of Masala incense, carrying marble chess games, ivory elephant figurines, and ornate ashtrays.

Foreigners in a new land, we aimlessly roamed the shopping centers, sitting at tables with Nasser, who enthusiastically rolled my miniature dice and made up rules with Joubin and me as we went along, buying fruits for our breakfasts, vegetables for our faithful burner, watching vendors pour pepper on clementines, watermelon, and corn, skipping in panic from my mother's sudden warnings lest we step on spit, or worse.

"Let's go to the Marriott," she often said.

Joubin's and my strides increased considerably at these suggestions. Welcomed by the hotel's polished marble floors, dazzling chandeliers, and lush plants, our ultimate destination was always to the pristine restrooms. To watch our mother freshen up there was like watching the same film in slow motion. She would take Joubin's hands in hers, passing them through the clear water that reflected the bright light, carefully lathering their fingers, gently submerging them in the stream that flowed from the shiny faucet, even after all the suds had been rinsed away. Each drop she would then pat dry. In front of the grand mirror, she would take out her pink comb, the one she had carried in her purse for as long as I could remember, and pass it through her long, wavy black hair. Our leisurely walk back to the others signaled the close of our brief and cherished moments at the Marriott.

"Can we wash our hands again?" Joubin often asked minutes later. And he would always hear, "Another day."

When my parents couldn't fill, or tolerate, the idle hours any longer, we returned to the steps of the embassies, back to the wait among countless other faces painted as if they were at a clinic, anticipating their diagnoses.

"We still have no information," the American clerk said, adjusting his glasses. "We don't have access to your files as yet." The immigration documents that my aunt had filed from the U.S. to its embassy in Iran were now lost somewhere in the piles of mess left by the hostage crisis.

During one of our walks with Hamid by our side, my attention wandered to a little boy not much older than Joubin. He was chewing and sucking on a piece of sugarcane and watching a man peel a tall stalk from his big stack of canes in a cart. What could that taste like? I wondered before we reached the street vendor, who was selling incense, socks, and packs of Chiclets chewing gum on one table. Hamid pointed to a free park bench across the street.

"You may want to consider renting a home until you wait for

your Visa," he said in a low voice when we sat down. Joubin rolled the brand-new green Hot Wheel that he had just received from my mother over the entire surface of the bench. When my parents didn't offer anything but empty faces, Hamid continued, "It makes much more sense than paying for the motel for weeks on end."

My father finally nodded, but my mother looked like an elephant had just stopped by to sit on her.

Not until we reached our motel room, behind the closed doors of our bathroom, did I hear my parents give voice to Hamid's suggestion.

"It's creating a sense of permanency," she said to my father.

"We won't be able to afford this room for much longer," he pointed out in a voice he thought Joubin and I couldn't hear. "We don't really have another choice."

The following two days, we toured residential neighborhoods, bouncing from house to house, searching and finding faults.

"Are we going to live here?" Joubin asked when we reached the doorstep of a white house.

"No, this is the home of one of Nasser's friends," our mother said as Nasser rang the loud doorbell.

Our gracious Pakistani hostess poured out the *doodh patti* that had been kept warm by the tea cozy and began a conversation with my mother in English. It was in that home that Joubin and I saw the familiar in our mother—her smiling eyes, her voice free of the weight that had leeched onto it for so long. We were seeing the mother we had had tea with in the living rooms back in Tehran, although, in the ones there, we hadn't had *doodh patti* or a curtain separating us from the men. Joubin and their seven-year-old son spent most of that hour spread on the gray-tiled floor, racing and crashing their Hot Wheels to giggles and laughter.

"Thank you for taking us to see your friends," my mother told Nasser on our way back to our motel. I hadn't known how much she needed to have tea in someone's living room.

"Will we have to sit behind a curtain in our house, too?" Joubin asked.

"No," Nasser said, smiling as he lightly mussed his hair. "Only some homes here have curtains up."

"WHAT DO YOU THINK?" my father asked my mother the next day, after seeing a house with a modest garden.

She looked at the ground and gave a half shrug and a nod that could easily have passed for either a "yes" or "no." After a couple of blocks of silent walking, my father said, "Let's have a picnic."

"A picnic?" my mother said, stopping in her tracks, her words storming through the air. "How can you even *think* of a picnic right now?"

"There's nothing we can do, Khandan," my father said.

"Khandan"— not "Khandan joon," or "Mamile," or any of the Farsi or German terms of endearment we were used to hearing.

"There has to be *something* we can do," she said with an audible lump forming in her throat. "I can't bear another six months of this."

We didn't go on a picnic, but we did manage to go to the movie theatre the next day. By far, our favorite nights of the week were

Thursdays, the only nights the theatre offered films in English rather than John Wayne films in Urdu. Of course, I didn't understand the words on either nights, but at least on Thursdays, my mother's whispers to me shed light on James Bond's every move, explained the course that led to Joan of Arc's fate that tied her to a pole. I carried Joan with me for a long time. It hadn't helped that, just before watching that film, I had discovered that my yellow Snow White wallet was missing. No words or gentle hugs my mother offered could relieve my pain at the loss of that precious fortune.

"My bird was in there," I said, barely managing the words.

"Which bird?" asked my mother, drying my tears.

"The tiny yellow glass bird Papaji had given me," I said, holding together the tip of my thumb and index finger to demonstrate how small it had been. "It was inside the coin pocket."

Under my mother's warm embrace, the pencil drawings of Papaji's birds appeared before me—his dainty birds, with fine features. At least they didn't tie me to a pole, I thought after a moment, and wiped away the drawings. I wanted to wipe away Joan too, but she wasn't going away. Neither was my mother's anguish over having to spend the next six months waiting for something that might or might not be granted to us.

During our fifth week in Pakistan, we waited as we always did for the morning knock on the door, in order to dismiss the cleaning attendant. This time, though, we were also waiting for a second knock—Hamid's.

Most of that day we spent inside our room, with breaks to play in the backyard.

"Do we use our Afghan passport or Iranian?" my mother asked Hamid.

"No, not the Afghan passports. Too risky now. Without Nasser or me, you won't be able to pull it off if someone ends up speaking to you in dialect. No, go with your Iranian passports."

"The kids are on my passport, and it's up to date, but Bahman's has expired," she said, opening my father's passport.

Hamid rubbed his cheeks up and down with his fingertips, his frown gaze fixed on the passports. "So you have two problems here—you need a new expiration date, and an entry stamp into Pakistan, before you can leave the country."

"Right," she said, pressing her lips into her knuckles.

"I don't know how we'll get around the expiration date, but I can get you an Iranian exit stamp," he said.

"How will we get an entry stamp into Pakistan, though?" my mother asked.

"I have some ideas, but first let's see what kind of tickets we can find to Germany."

I was determined not to let my thoughts be carried away.

BY LATE AFTERNOON, JOUBIN and I were leafing through pages of magnificent beaches, old architectural sites, and multitudes of happy and carefree people. Unaware of our parents' attempt to convince the travel agent that their Austrian driver's licenses were special visas to Germany, Joubin's attention drifted to a propped up model of a jet, while mine played with the temptation to step into one of the posters on the walls, any poster. Hamid's convincing words, supported by my parents' pretense of annoyance over the agent's confusion, won us tickets to Düsseldorf via Paris.

"Can we eat at Ali Baba's tonight?" Joubin asked.

Even before our father's "not tonight," I knew that we wouldn't be dining there. We hadn't—or anywhere else other than in our room, for two weeks.

My father's potato-onion-and-scrambled-egg dish tasted better than ever that night, perfect with *naan*, cucumbers, and *doodh patti*.

"I'll pick up the stamp tomorrow," Hamid said, placing his cup on our little dresser as he headed to the door.

A WRINKLED LITTLE PAPER BAG rested on our little table the next day. Out of it, Hamid pulled out a stamp and ink pad. "So you have Iran's exit stamp now. All you need is Pakistan's entry stamp."

My father's face rested in his palm. Hamid continued, "If you go to India, then fly back into Pakistan, to Karachi, since your departure is from there. . . ."

"Won't India ask why we don't have an entry stamp into Pakistan?" my mother asked.

"The guards at the border I'm going to take you to aren't that well trained."

"So we'll have an exit stamp and entry stamp," my father said, nodding, the tension leaving his face.

"They may not even notice your expiration date at this border," Hamid said, "but you'll still need a valid passport at the airport."

"These numbers can be altered," said my mother, drawing out her words as she studied the ones on my father's passport. All our heads turned to her. She never looked up from her trance. "It's tricky, though. I have to change both the Farsi numbers as well as the European numbers, and their expiration dates have to match both the lunar and the Gregorian calendars."

Hamid's hands went into the air, as if he was being arrested. "This part, I won't be able to help you with," he said, shaking his head.

"No, no, *I* can do this," she said mildly, finally lifting her head towards Hamid. "I used to work for the Iranian Embassy in Austria. I validated this passport by hand. It's in my own handwriting. I just have to figure out how to shape the numbers. If I turn this zero into a one. . . ."

"May I?" asked Hamid, reaching for the passport. "Hmm," he said, nodding, before he handed it back to her. My father had been leaning over her shoulders for a better look when she asked him, "What do you think?"

"Yeah," he said, almost sure.

"Do you have a black marker?" she asked Hamid.

"You're going to do it now?" asked my father.

"If we're okay to do this, I can do it now," she said, looking like she was about to perform an unwanted surgery with the marker.

Joubin and I sat on our bed, awaiting the next move, word, or expression. I knew that this went against everything they had taught us, that it was far worse than my failed attempt to forge my mother's signature on a letter my beloved teacher sent home when she had mistaken my mistimed whisper to Lili as cheating on an exam.

I also knew that we were running out of money, and that my mother needed to reach Germany more than any of us.

My parents' eyes moved to Hamid, who didn't want them on him, so they turned back to each other. My father's nod, then my mother's, initiated the operation. She picked up the marker and leaned forward. Determined not to distract her from this dreaded task, no one made a sound. Nothing but her hand was in motion, first practicing on scrap paper, then mimicking her subtle movements in mid air, before her marker touched the pages of my father's passport, at which point I forgot to breathe for a few seconds.

She leaned back and considered her work, looking up for opinions. Hamid and my father stepped closer.

"Pretty good," Hamid said. "It should work. When do you want to do this?"

"As soon a possible," my father said, looking to her. She nodded accordingly.

"Tomorrow morning, we go to the Indian embassy to get you a visa. It will only take a day or two."

W E WERE ONE OF the first to be seen at the embassy the following morning. Hamid had been right. All that was expected from us in order to acquire the visa was a cholera vaccine, which we quickly received after having lunch at Ali Baba, a special treat from Hamid and Nasser. Could it really be our last visit there? Would the owner miss us and wonder what had happened to us? I wondered, barely daring to entertain that possibility, then decided not to think about it any further.

Yet unlike the other times, we were making progress. The following day, we stood before a clerk whose sheer green scarf was loosely draped around her hair and shoulders. After a quick glance at our vaccination documents, she reached for her ink box. The thumping sound, as she stamped our passports, rang into my ears. A sound that ruled. Irrevocable.

"It's best to be at the border early, before it gets too crowded," Hamid said that afternoon on the walk back to our motel. "It may be better to leave for Lahore tonight and catch a taxi to the border early in the morning."

"We don't have much to pack, so we can be ready quickly," my mother said.

An hour later, Nasser bent down to my eye level. "Have a great time in Germany."

What? You're not coming along? I thought.

"I'm going to miss our dice games," he continued.

"Yes," I managed to say. My "thank you" got stuck in my throat, and I was intent on making it through that farewell without tears, so I bobbed my head in smiles instead. How had I missed it? Why wasn't he coming with us? A gnawing pain was building in my chest. I fought my watery eyes by wiping away the streams of memories and expressions of gratitude that were flooding my mind.

"Hey, little guy," he said to Joubin, mussing up his hair. "Don't forget your little cars!"

The remaining exclamations of good wishes and thanks I overheard, as I adjusted and readjusted the corner of our bed-spread, threw me into dread of the same scene we'd have to face with Hamid the next morning.

"The taxi's here," Nasser called out. "Let's go."

CHAPTER SIX

I PREFERRED LAHORE AT dawn. Although I could hear the sound of our engine, the birds, and the wind from the open window of our taxi, it still felt like complete silence compared to the usual rumble and chaos of cars and mini buses honking for the sake of honking. The wind blew a strand of hair from my ponytail into my face, and I let it. The emerging promise of a new day managed to prevail over my tired body and foggy mind.

Hamid paid the taxi driver, whose rear view mirror was adorned with a dangling Pakistani flag, the white star and moon on green waving from side to side, bidding us farewell.

We descended onto a busy path carrying travelers, some by car and others on foot.

"Just stay in the crowd," Hamid said, looking into the distance.

"Right," my father said, nodding.

"You need to go before it gets too crowded," Hamid said again, eyeing a large family that was passing us.

My father stood motionless for a few seconds before he extended his arms wide. "Hamid jan," he said, and held him close in a firm embrace.

I turned away, my eyes scanning the ground, looking for something, it didn't matter what, and heard Hamid say, "May God be with you," in a low voice.

"There're no words to thank you," my mother said. Exactly, I thought as I ran my foot back and forth over the lone pebble beneath my sole. Thank you for saving us from getting killed—three times? Thank you for taking us to the movies? Thank you for finding a way to Germany? Thank you for Ali B. . . .

"Keep well," Hamid said, directly looking at Joubin and me, saluting in midair.

My lungs were heavy, my forehead still spinning with words, my voice empty of sound; Joubin smiled and waved.

"*Merci*," I finally heard myself say. No amount of gargling with salt water or happy news could relieve the ache in my throat.

"Go, it's getting crowded," he said to my father with a nod towards the border.

Yes, let's go, I agreed. We merged with the foot traffic, and I defied my vows not to look back at Hamid, catching glimpses of him still standing where we had left him, with crossed arms, among the young and old bearing their belongings in wrapped cloths, oversized nylon sacs, and plastic baskets.

We inched our way toward the uniformed men. *Hate borders*, I said to myself, feeling my pulse in my stomach. What if he notices? I thought when the guard reached for the passports in my father's hand. I felt nauseous. What if my mother had used the wrong kind of pen? I wished I could be asleep.

Yet much like anticipating the pain of a shot in a doctor's office, it was over before I knew it. The guard waved us past like a herd of sheep. I felt my heart beat faster.

I couldn't see Hamid through the bodies moving around me, but my father's raised arm towards our friend told me that he was still waiting, back in Pakistan.

"We're in India now?" I asked my father.

"Not yet," he answered. "It's ahead. A bit of a walk still."

"So we're still in Pakistan?"

"No," he said quietly, "it's no-man's land."

No-man's land?

Had it not been barren and gated, I would have liked to live in a no-man's land, I thought. In my visions of leaving Pakistan, my parents' faces had been more animated and joyful, yet like so many of my other imaginings, the scenes in my head were to belong to a different story. What I was forgetting was that, by leaving Pakistan, we were also leaving behind the sanctuary of that piece of U.N. paper my father had been keeping close in his pocket every day, which was now rendering us powerless should we be discovered as escapees from Iran.

"Are we in India yet?" Joubin asked.

"Not yet," my mother said. "A little farther."

Our walk on the dusty path without our trusted friends, surrounded by faces and tongues that were foreign, stretched the *far* in "farther."

Perhaps a half hour later, I was finally able to see the tip of a turban peeking over the crowd in the distance. Like a timer, my heart set itself into heavy beats again as we approached the Indian border. The bearded guard shouted something to another guard as he was questioning a frail old man standing before us.

"Hello, sir," my father said to the guard in English as he handed him our passports.

"Hello," the guard said blankly, looking down at our booklets.

The Pakistani guard let us through, I said silently to the bearded man with the turban, as he quickly flipped through the pages. He threw me a quick glance. My heart stopped. Could he hear me?

"Thank you," he said, returning our passports to my father.

Eight steps into India, I finally caught sight of a tinge of brightness that passed across my parents' eyes, and I breathed easier.

"G OL KAGHAZI!" my mother exclaimed from the back seat of the taxi ride to Amritsar Airport.

"You scared me," my father said from the front seat. "The poor driver nearly jumped out of his skin, too."

I laughed.

"No, he didn't," she said with a chuckle. "Look, they're so beautiful. Do you know how hard it is to grow these in the gardens back home?"

In my mind, I kept replaying our startled expressions and laughed more.

"I can't believe it," she continued. "In Tehran, they require such special care, and here they're just growing wild in the street."

I couldn't stop laughing.

"Look at that palace!" Joubin cried out, as we were nearing a gold temple. "Is that where their king lives?"

"No, but it's a beautiful temple, isn't it?" my father said.

"Do you have to swim to get to it?"

"There's a passage, see?" I said to him.

"Do you think Nasser and Hamid will visit us in Germany?" I asked my mother an hour later at the small airport, while we sat on the hard metal chairs awaiting my father's return from the ticket agent.

"It'd be nice if they could," she said, smiling.

"We can't get tickets to New Delhi from here. I have to go to a travel agent in town," said my father when he rejoined us.

"...In town?" my mother said.

"I think it'll be quicker and easier if you wait here," he said in a rushed voice.

"Do you know where you're going?" she asked, her face clouding over.

"I'll take a taxi."

Fortunately for my brother, his Hot Wheels pulled him into his own world. I had my dice, but I didn't want to remove them from the pouch Nooshin joon had knitted for me.

The first two hours were what my mother and I expected to wait. Joubin and I filled the time with games of "Twenty Questions" and raised ones of our own, like "Does Germany look like Vienna?" "How come they don't have anything to eat here?" and "How can they have a castle like that and an airport like this?"

"Let's walk around a bit," our mother said, impatience building in her voice. We strolled in the direction her gaze had been anchored on that past hour, the end of the somber hall.

After our two-minute adventure, Joubin asked, "Can we look at the airplanes?"

We looked out the cloudy terminal windows, saw two small, stationary planes, and returned to the metal seats to sit by our mother.

"Do you think we'll run into Julia on a Strassenbahn, by chance? Or maybe Susan?"

My mother almost smiled and shrugged. "Don't know about Julia, but I'll be able to get Susan's address. Hopefully, we'll be able to go for a visit."

"Really?" I said, eyes wide. Susan was not only one of my classmates who had left Iran during the Revolution, our parents were also longtime friends from their Vienna days.

"Why isn't he coming?" my mother said finally after the third hour had come and gone.

"Maybe," I said, "there's a lot of traffic," a response that only elicited a distracted nod.

Or maybe some secret police followed us from the border this morning, I said to myself, *and has stopped him somewhere to question him. Maybe that's why it was so easy to leave Pakistan and enter India.*

"You know how crazy people drive, always cutting in," I said. "He's just stuck in traffic."

Or lying in some car wreck or hospital.

"I think that plane moved," Joubin said from the window.

"Right," I said.

"It did," he said, squinting. "Just a little."

"Where do you think Layla is now?" I asked my mother.

Probably still in Lahore," my mother said.

"Wish she was here now," I said. Her faraway gaze dissipated my questions, adding an extra sixty seconds to each minute we spent within those lifeless walls. Wish Nasser was here too, I thought. He would no doubt've surprised us with a treat, made up some silly game to play, or talked to us.

"Why aren't there any planes that move?" Joubin asked.

"I think our flight is the only one that's leaving here today," our mother said with a sigh.

By THE FOURTH HOUR, Joubin and I were no longer exchanging any words with our mother. Her mouth had been covered with her fist for most of that hour, her worry-filled eyes no doubt painting scenarios of her own while my stomach churned with my own doubts of seeing my father again.

"We have forty-five minutes before our plane leaves," she said, visibly constraining the panic in her voice. "Let's walk down the hall again."

Thirty minutes later, we saw my father rushing towards us.

"I thought something *happened* to you," my mother said, her voice heavy as lead.

"Nothing happened. Traffic and long queues to see the agent," he said quickly. "Our flight's about to take off. Kids, let's run."

His words sent us all flying towards the gate and into the air.

ALL CITIES SHOULD BE entered from above at night, I thought, looking down from my window seat at the dazzling lights pulling me down to the vast ornamented land. I debated waking my mother up to show her what lay below, although I knew that she wasn't really sleeping.

"Oh, look," I heard Joubin say from a couple of rows back.

Good, at least *they're* seeing it, I said to myself, and for the remainder of our landing I pressed as close to the window as my seatbelt allowed.

The New Delhi Airport was swarming with the bright colors of saris and gold bangles. Clusters of onlookers with flowers at hand stood by the gates we passed, eyes searching for faces they awaited. It reminded me of the times in Iran when we used to pick up our visitors from abroad. The airport would be swarming with groups of families, immediate and extended, accompanied by friends and their families—all waiting to greet their loved ones with floral arrangements.

I was always drawn in by the exclamations of delight of reunited strangers, their tight embraces, and joyful weeping that inevitably brought me to tears as well.

"We should always fly from this airport," Joubin said, bringing a half smile to our mother's face.

"Are you crying?" Joubin asked me next.

"No!"

From the taxi, I took in images of buildings and pavements that were somewhat more modern than the ones we had seen in Pakistan. I was intrigued by a spotlit temple that we were approaching.

"Bahman, the driver. . . ." said my mother in alarm.

"I know," my father said calmly from the front passenger seat, without moving his head. "I'm watching the road in case I need to steer."

"What happened?" I asked my mother.

"The driver just let go of his steering wheel," she answered, gaze unmoving.

"Why?" I said.

"To bring his hands together," she said impatiently. "He's showing respect to the temple we just passed."

For the remainder of our taxi ride, my parents and I saw New Delhi from the front window; nobody dared look to the side.

We were soon nearing another temple. Is he going do it again now? I wondered.

My father's hand moved closer to the steering wheel. My eyes were fixed on the driver. Are there more accidents in front of temples? I wondered after the driver bowed his head, palms together, before calmly resuming control of his wheel again.

"He *is* good at it," I said.

My parents had no comments. Their necks and hawk-like eyes didn't waver.

We were greeted at the hotel by a man in a white shirt and tie. Though not a large hotel, its furnishings reminded us of more modern times, its blue carpets stain-free and, above all, clean. Fortunately, our room shared the same characteristics.

"A real bathroom!" Joubin said with excitement. "It even has a tub and everything."

"Let's quickly wash our hands and get a bite to eat," our mother said, her bright face reflecting in the clear and flawless mirror.

After we dined at a fish 'n' chips restaurant, my mother stopped at a shoe store. "Can't go to Germany with sandals in the middle of December," she said. While she looked at a pair of brown loafers, my father and I watched Joubin heavily engrossed in a video game at an electronic store two doors down.

"What did you say to him?" I asked my father, who had exchanged a couple of English words with the store owner.

"I asked him if he was closing. He is, but he wants Joubin to continue his game," he said, arms crossed, smiling, his voice soft.

Our walk back to our hotel in the night-lit streets, in anticipation of our flight to Germany the next morning, felt like we were walking in a dream. But as in all dreams, we were sidetracked by real life, the life of groups of children who lived in cardboard boxes, who surrounded us with stretched-out hands and sad eyes, uttering words we didn't understand yet knew were speaking of pain.

When it was my turn to bathe before bed, I stood in the middle of the white-tiled bathroom for a few moments to simply look at the tub, the shower nozzle, the white towels, and the clear mirror. I loved the fresh aroma of the hotel shampoo that still lingered in the air from my brother's bath.

The high pressure of the warm water gushing over my head reawakened images of the dust particles that had latched on to our hair for weeks after our days in the desert, stubbornly resisting the trickling water of our previous motels, their cracked walls, and our aimless walks in wait of visas. With my foot, I directed the soapy water around my feet towards the drain, and watched the circling suds disappear through the little holes. Yet neither the pounding water nor the fresh scented shampoo were having any effect on washing away the anguished voices of those street children who had haunted me all the way back to our room.

By ten o'clock that evening, an embarrassed hotel attendant told us that our neighbors had complained about the sound of our hairdryer.

"It's *your* hair dryer," my father told him in English.

"Yes, but they say it's been on for the past two hours," the attendant said, smiling.

"We have very thick hair," my father said with a friendly shrug—thick hair that had been frizzy for six weeks.

"Yes, Karachi," my father answered the ticket agent at the airport the following morning. "Karachi, Paris, Düsseldorf."

Maybe this time, I thought.

Our ascent into the air towards Karachi ended our twenty-four-hour stay in India.

"I thought we were going to Germany," Joubin said on the airplane.

"We are," my mother said. "We're just changing planes in Karachi. From there we'll fly to Paris. Then we'll connect to our Düsseldorf flight."

"Three airplanes!" Joubin said holding the same number of little fingers up.

Our delay on the runway had our parents looking at their watches every few minutes, exchanging anxious looks.

"I'M SORRY, SIR, YOUR flight has left," said the Air France ticket agent. "The next one is in the evening."

"That's ten hours from now," my mother said as we roamed in search of seats for the long day before us. The few we found were occupied by other passengers, who looked like they hadn't slept much.

"Excuse me," my father said, when we found ourselves back at the same ticket agent's counter. "Is there anywhere besides the floor that we can pass these ten hours with our children?"

The agent brushed her hair behind her ears, looked at Joubin and me, and said, "Wait one moment, please." She raised a telephone receiver to her ear and spoke in Hindi for a minute before saying, "Sir, we will put you up at the Taj Mahal Hotel during your wait for tonight's flight. A taxi will take you there and back."

Wide-eyed, my parents must have expressed five versions of "thank you."

We spent our last hours in Pakistan in a palace the likes of which I had only seen in Tehran's finest hotels. Whether the Hyatt, Sheraton, or any other, we'd always looked forward to the dinners, the weddings, or my father's meetings I was lucky enough to attend one or two times.

He always ordered a tall glass of tomato juice with a leafy celery stick and a slice of lemon. My order never changed either: "Cherry compote, please." It was only during those informal business meetings that my compote didn't disappear in minutes. After every spoonful of cherry, I adjusted my skirt or hair, leaned back against my leather chair, and passed my time doing what I loved most—people watching.

"HERE ARE THE KEYS to your rooms," the hotel clerk said to my father.

"Oh, we only need one, thank you," he said, returning one of the keys.

"Is this Pakistan?" Joubin asked, when we were walking towards the elevators.

"Yes," said our father. "We're in Karachi. It's another city in Pakistan."

"Why didn't we just come here from the beginning?"

"Because it wasn't the part of Pakistan, or Karachi, we could afford," he answered, laughing. "This hotel is a gift from Air France. Enjoy it."

We did—every inch of the double suite, outfitted with the finest furnishings.

"Are you hungry?" he asked.

"Yes!" Joubin and I said, tossing aside the black folder that listed all the movie selections that were at our service.

"You can just live here," Joubin said, as we passed the Taj Mahal's fine stores and dining areas. "You can get your hair cut here, then go to that fancy place there and buy a purse, and go upstairs to see your movie, then come back down and eat at this restaurant, and for dinner go to the other restaurant we saw before. . . ."

"We're only staying here for a few hours," I reminded him.

"I know," he said. "I'm just saying *if* we stayed here, we wouldn't ever have to go outside."

Palace food, I thought, when our waiter decorated our white tablecloth with dishes of orange-colored chicken skewers on rice, ornately presented with lemon slices, parsley, and *naan*.

"Can we watch a movie when we go back upstairs?" Joubin asked.

"I think we'll take a nap," our mother said. "We have a long trip ahead."

"Does Germany look like Pakistan? *This* Pakistan?"

"No," she told him. "It's different. Do you remember when we visited Vienna? You were two."

"I had the 'Willie' popsicle," he said, nodding. We had reminisced about those popsicles so often, it was probably one of the few memories he retained of our visit to Austria.

"Right. Well, it's more like Vienna, but still different."

"But they'll still have the popsicles, right?"

"If not "Willie,' something like it, I'm sure."

"Something like it" gave way to Joubin's own flavor dreams: "bubble gum with pieces of rainbow gum," "purple and pink sour ice cream," "chocolate and yellow ice cream," and—why not?— "gummy bear ice cream."

"Do we have to sleep now?" Joubin asked, when we had returned to our room after lunch.

It did seem a waste to miss out on the luxury, but the darkened room called for rest, and as it turned out, it seemed that we were more tired than we had realized. The ringing telephone forced us awake hours later, allowing enough time for a quick, luxurious shower.

"My shirt!" said Joubin with bright eyes, grabbing the checkered shirt that our mother was taking out of our little tan bag.

"I didn't know you brought my shirt and vest," I said, holding my favorite brown skirt to my waist.

"We saved these for when we entered Germany," she said.

Why had I not even wondered why we never opened that small bag during our entire trip?

BEFORE WE BOARDED THE flight that divided my father and me from Joubin and my mother by six rows, my father had pulled Joubin and me aside. "From now on, you don't have to be careful about holding hands with me in public. And I can squeeze and hug you again like I always have," he said, wrapping us in his arms, making us laugh in the midst of our suffocation, reminding us that he was Abbas joon's son after all. Kisses later, he looked like a mixture of Michael Landon in the final moments of an episode of *Little House on the Prairie* and John Travolta about to embark on his final stride.

I felt I had finally been reunited with Roya, our memories one and the same. I was wearing the peach cotton shirt I used to wear only at parties in Tehran, accompanied by its brown skirt and vest. My arm remained folded over my father's for most of the flight, occasionally taking a break for food service or when the flight attendant handed him a form to be filled out.

"What does that mean?" I asked him, pointing to a word above an empty box.

"Suggestions," he said.

"What did you suggest?"

"Nothing. I asked a question instead."

"What?"

He placed his pen down and read: "Why did you (France) do this to us (the Iranian people)?"

It was common knowledge in Iran that, without the invitation from French President Valéry Giscard d'Estaing calling Khomeini to live in his country in 1978, the Ayatollah would not have been able to mastermind the Islamic Revolution from his home in the Paris suburbs and hold regular meetings with journalists under the watchful eye of France. I hadn't forgotten the TV images of Khomeini's arrival on Iranian soil in 1979, being escorted down the airplane steps, his elbow gently supported by an Air France pilot.

"You wanna visit the pilot?" Joubin asked, coming up to our

seats. His eyes were bright with excitement. "The flight attendant is gonna take us."

"No, you go," I said, and traveled back to 1979, the riots of thousands of protestors screaming death wishes to the Shah, to America, to Israel, shouts that lasted well beyond 1979. Memories of Ayatollah Khomeini crept before me: the face that never smiled, the hand that waved up and down, as if playing with an invisible yo-yo, while the crowds cheered him on, carrying the fainted among them. . . .

I HADN'T SEEN SO MANY European faces in one place for years. The Paris airport was flooded with fair people in transit. For six weeks we had stood out palely among our neighbors; now we stood out as dark foreigners. My father's recounting of a story from my childhood rushed back to me.

"Oh, what big dark eyes you have. Did you forget to wash them this morning?" an old man had asked on a Strassenbahn in Vienna when I was two years old. My father was yet to forgive the comment the old man had probably meant as a compliment. Ei ther way, it was one comment too many, making him vow never to return to Austria after we left Vienna in 1976.

During the two-hour delay, we strolled through the duty-free stores in the connecting-flight area. My father tried on several sunglasses, igniting his Bond impersonations, which made Joubin and me giggle and my mother roll her eyes in annoyance. He also tried a few hats, which amused my mother even less. Yet Joubin and my giggles continued to the seats in the waiting area as he recounted jokes we'd already heard.

"How can you *joke* at a time like this?" she asked finally, her face as stormy as her voice.

"A time like what?" my father replied, opening his hands.

My mother's knuckles pressed harder against her lips as our flight number was announced over the main speakers.

CHAPTER SEVEN

Butterflies fluttered through my chest and stomach as the plane descended. The little patches of brown squares and green rectangles from above slowly turned into neighborhoods and roofs, roads and highways, bearing what seemed like an array of moving Hot Wheels filled with passengers going about their day, oblivious to our descending plane and the lives it was carrying. We'll be one of those cars soon, I thought.

We lagged behind the line of commuters; "No, please, after you," we said to whoever wanted to honor our place in line. "We have time. Won't you go ahead of us, please?" we added, assuring that we'd be the last remaining travelers.

"During our entire trip—the desert, in Pakistan, India—I wasn't as terrified as I am right now," my mother said to my father in a hushed voice.

"Now?" he said. "Why are you so worried?"

"*Why*? 'Cause I know Germans! And so do you! You know how they stick to rules and regulations." She whispered the rest of her sentence, hoping Joubin and I wouldn't hear. "What if they don't accept us? They can send us back to Iran. What will we do then?"

"They won't," he said calmly.

"How do you know? How can you not be concerned? How do you just brush things off like that?"

"Because," he answered calmly, "when I called Pari joon back in Iran, I told her in code that I had heard our friend Bahman and his family were coming for a visit, and that they'd probably appreciate her help. I also asked her to send me Ahmad's poem." (The "Tablet of Ahmad" is a Bahá'í prayer offered at difficult times.) "A few days later, she called and told me that she had sent the poem by air through registered mail. That's when I knew we'd reach safety."

"How do you know that's enough?" she said, her voice calm this time.

"I know."

Our turn came. We were the only ones left in that big hall. Sheepishly, we walked towards the glass passport control counter, where a pale, blonde young man reached for our passports and tickets.

"*Guten Tag*," he said in an official tone.

"*Guten Tag*," my parents said together as the agent looked

through our passports. He turned the pages of one booklet, scanning each page carefully, then flipped back to the first page.

"You're not finding a visa because we don't have one," my father said.

What? I wanted to call out. My mind began to race faster than my heart.

"We're seeking asylum," my father said calmly.

The young agent continued to stare at my father; it made me feel we were the Von Trapp family, in the middle of a cathedral cemetery, at the mercy of Rolph's dilemma. Finally, the agent called out to one of his colleagues to take his position and waved for us to follow him. From the second-floor glass window, we could see the reunited families on the other side of Passport Control. A tall man in a navy jacket and chapeau stood below, alone, looking up in our direction. It's him, I thought, Pari joon's brother. And suddenly, she was there too, her voice washing over me like a wave, her chant as loud as the announcements that were flying over the speakers.

"*Verstehst du Deutch?*" a middle aged man in a blue-striped tie asked me in German, after we were presented to him.

"*Ya, Ich verstehe,*" I answered, wanting to impress. "*Ich bin in Wien geboren.*"

"Come, you can sit here at this desk," he continued, as he cleared away the loose papers that lay in a pile. "Frau Schmidt, would you get us some markers, please?"

He took out three blank sheets of paper and placed them in front of me, adding the markers Frau Schmidt handed to him. "Do you think your brother wants to draw, too?" he asked, looking at Joubin's sleepy face.

"He doesn't like to do anything when he looks like that," I told him.

"If your son would like, he can lie down there," he said to my mother, pointing to the gray sofa.

"Thank you," my mother said, directing Joubin towards his makeshift bed.

The middle-aged man introduced himself as Herr Meyer. He pointed to another man, similar in age, who wore thick, brown-framed glasses, sitting behind a typewriter. "My colleague will record our conversation," he said dryly. "Now, I understand that you have entered Germany without a visa."

"Yes," my father said, initiating the clicks of the typewriter. "We escaped from Iran six weeks ago, and we've finally reached here to seek refugee status from Germany."

"Why did you escape from Iran?" he asked, in a cool voice.

"We're Bahá'ís."

"And?"

"And the persecutions of Bahá'ís have intensified since the Revolution."

"Which means?"

"Which means," my father continued in a firm but soft voice, "that, at any moment, our homes could be broken into by guards, calling for our arrests, which means torture and waiting to see what follows—prison, execution, or release!"

The clicking sounds stopped, giving time for a brief exchange of raised eyebrows between the German colleagues. My mother picked up the rest of the conversation.

"We had to pull our children out of school. Our daughter went to the Deutsche Schule in Tehran, before it was turned into an Iranian Public School. Then my husband was threatened at work."

"What was your position?" asked Herr Meyer.

"I was a director in a carpet manufacturing company," my father said. "I was fired for not recanting my Faith and was expected to pay back three years of salary, which we didn't have."

"When did you decide to leave?"

"I was receiving threats and knew that it was a matter of time before they arrested me. We had to leave. Didn't have much choice, I couldn't let my kids grow up there. . . . Between the threats and the bombings, we were running out of places to hide."

During the director's endless questions, which were receiving endless answers, Frau Schmidt disappeared a while and returned with a bag of potato chips, two bananas, Haribo Gummibärchen, and a cup of apple juice. She held them up, getting my mother's attention for approval before placing them beside my drawing and whispering, "You must be hungry by now."

"*Vielen Dank!*" I said with the brightest smile I could manage.

"I'll keep your brother's on my desk for when he wakes up," Frau Schmidt said.

"*Gute idee!*" I said, nodding. "*Danke schön.*"

"The first guard at the Iran–Pakistan border didn't let us leave," my father was saying when I pulled open the bag of Gummy Bears, releasing the fruity aroma that made me feel like I was a pre-schooler in Vienna again, on my way to play ball in the park with my father.

"Our truck was damaged, and we had to wait half a day in the open desert for another truck to take us to a village."

I think the clear ones are pineapple, I thought, picking them out of the colorful mix. They had always been my favorite.

"No, through the river, we had the engine off. The driver pushed the truck."

"*Mensch!*" the officer behind the typewriter exclaimed.

Maybe Joubin will like the orange flavor. I'll keep those for him.

"What we can do is give you a three-month visa," Herr Meyer said, breathing a heavy sigh as he leaned forward on his desk. "And then you can renew it later."

"Herr Meyer," my father said, moving to the edge of his seat. "We kindly seek refugee status."

"Your kids are tired," said Herr Meyer, resting his clenched fist on his desk. "Why go through this lengthy procedure? Just come back in three months and renew your visa."

"The kids are fine," my mother said, her voice starting to break. "You don't know what it's been like, Herr Meyer."

I looked back at my airplane drawing and continued to color it green.

"But why refugee status? You'll have to go to a refugee camp. Do you really want that?"

"My uncle lives here," my father said. "He's a professor at a university here. He's outside, downstairs. He's here."

Herr Meyer turned to Frau Schmidt, who hadn't done any typing, writing, or much else from the time she had brought me snacks. "Page him."

My parents took turns recounting the fate of some of the Bahá'ís we had known in Iran, before the office door opened. Directly behind a German officer stood my father's uncle. Tall and gray, he held his crisp chapeau and navy leather gloves in his hand. He reminded me of Abbas joon, not in his face, but in the way he held himself, erect, after-shaved, his checkered gray scarf neatly and discreetly showing from under his coat, not a wrinkle or unwanted piece of lint in sight.

My father rose from his seat and, with open arms, embraced his handsome uncle before he was invited to sit down.

Herr Meyer repeated the offer of the three-month visa, mostly looking in my great-uncle's direction, who in turn asked his nephew: "Isn't that good?"

"No, Dai jan," my father said, keeping his gaze on the typewriter. "We need refugee status."

"Why refugee?" asked Herr Meyer.

"Herr Meyer, my wife and I haven't slept a single restful night in over three months. I ask you from the bottom of my heart, please, grant us refugee status."

I was now looking much like Frau Schmidt, both of us waiting for the next word to drop, hopefully from Herr Meyer, who kept tapping his lips with his joined index fingers and clasped fist.

The silence was broken by my great-uncle. "Herr Meyer, if I may, I am willing to act as their guardian. They can live with me, under my care."

All eyes shifted back to Herr Meyer, who after a moment, finally leaned forward and said, "You are now under the protection of Germany. Welcome to my country."

My mother released a flood of tears. My father rose and, with both hands reached for Herr Meyer's, shaking it firmly, then clasped his great-uncle in another hearty embrace.

"Now, I need to make this clear—as refugees, you will present yourself to a court in Düsseldorf once a week. You will update all your health statuses, and you will not be permitted outside the city limits."

Herr Director's sobering words subdued the celebratory hugs, binding my parents to nods of understanding.

"*Daí jan*, this will take a while. We'll take a taxi to you when we're done here," my father said. "Thank you!"

Our silver-haired uncle rose from his seat and, in keeping with his elegance, directed a little wink at me. "We'll see you at home."

"Yes," I nodded, barely feeling my feet on the ground. I sat back down and continued the finishing touches on my second drawing of a house surrounded by snow-topped mountains, a stream that found its way from the hills towards the front of the house, two birds flying over the cotton-ball-looking trees, and two over the mountain top.

"Are these for me?" Herr Meyer asked when I handed him my two drawings. He paused and studied my illustrations. "You want to sign and date it?"

I returned to my desk and wrote: *Roya, 16 December 1981.*

"*Toll!*" Herr Meyer said, collecting pushpins from his drawer. He pinned up the drawings next to each other on the wall behind his desk: my house with the mountainous landscape, next to my green airplane that was releasing seven bombs.

"Golbakht!" I call, and don't hear her answer.
I run back to the land of sands and see no trace.
Have I killed her
or drowned her in the well of dust?
My tears are forming a stream of mud.
Her giggles haunting the heavy air,
robbing me of any desire to move.

Can you see me? she asks me.

FREEDOM

PART ONE

THE WOMAN RUNS THROUGH the dry forest grounds, hearing her own gasping echoes as her black cloak ripples behind her in velvet.

If she reaches her friend, she'll be safe.

She stops to catch her breath, leaning against Narvan, the elm. "He's coming," it tells her, so she keeps running.

Hours deeper into the forest, the reverberating sounds of Deev still follow her through trails of faded bushes that were once green. She slows her pace, clutching her cloak, and collapses onto the ground. Breathless, she turns on her back and faces the solemn gray clouds.

"Where did you fly to?" she murmurs to herself as her eyes search the naked trees that stand over her.

"Run!" says Sarv, the four-thousand-year-old pine, the only one that still stands upright. The Deev's roars crawl up her spine. Her friend is not much further ahead. The woman lifts herself and darts through the rays of light that pierce the gaps in the giant, tawny leaves.

A bone-chilling wind surpasses her. She turns to its hissing voice and wraps her cloak tightly around herself. She hears and sees her panting breaths dance wildly around her. The sounds of the crushing leaves beneath her steps grow louder the farther she moves into the gray woods.

Suddenly, she loses her hold on the ground and falls heavy on her back. "Black ice?" she says, as she touches the frozen earth, eyeing the bark and pale branches. The beginnings of ice pellets peck her face. "Can't be," she mutters, pulling the large hood over her head.

Like a ferocious animal, she plows through the brown bushes, past the silhouettes of trees stretched among their roots.

She cannot feel her legs move toward her friend, only her wild heart.

"What's happening here?" she asks her friend, holding its deformed trunk. Its strong sculpted arms, which have always cradled her to sleep, now lie lifeless on a sheet of ice.

"Dear one," the oak whispers.

"What sorcery is this?" she asks. "It has to be Zahhak's work."

"Maybe," the oak says with labored breath.

"That would mean his powers have doubled since his return

from Mount Damavand?"

"Rostam believes this to be the work of the Hayulah."

"The Hayulah?" the woman says. "Where is Rostam now?"

"He's gone—rode in search of the Hayulah. To break the spell."

"Where?"

"Don't know," whispers the oak. "If there's anyone that can defeat the Hayulah, it'll be him. But until he does, the ice storms are to reign over us."

A loud crack tears the sky, and the woman leaps aside moments before a heavy branch crashes on the ground.

"Beed!" the woman screams, running towards the willow.

She passes her hands over the missing limbs of the willow.

"He comes," the oak suddenly says wildly. "You must go!"

"I'll hide inside you," she says, running back to the oak.

"You can't!"

"But I always do," she cries, and falls to her knees.

"No! Get up!" the oak says sharply. "I can't! My senses are numb. I can't move a single limb. Run!"

The woman folds her hands over one of the oak's limp branches, her wet face hidden under her cloak.

"I say *run*! Do you *hear* me?" The oak has matched the Deev's thundering howls.

The woman doesn't move.

"You'll be ripped into pieces. Get up, I tell you!"

"Enough!" Her words rip through the air. "I've been running for more than a century. How long will you have me hiding from the Deev?"

"When Rostam returns—"

"Rostam?" cries the woman in anger. "Where was Rostam all these years? He knew, he saw, yet he always steered his horse down another path. Your Rostam doesn't fight for me! Let it be done!"

She lets go of the branch she has been nursing and faces in the direction of the screeching sounds.

"*Come!*" she screams, venom building in her voice.

"*No!*" The oak's bellow has shaken the ground. "If I had any strength in my limbs, I'd throw you across the forest right now. I say *run!*"

She holds her position, tears flowing down her chin.

"Please," the oak says, this time in a faint voice. "I won't be able to bear it." Out of breath, it pleads further, "*Please. . .* Run."

"Wait," the woman says, seizing the oak's trunk. "You have to hold on! I'll find your Rostam and bring him back. He'll break this spell."

"No!" the oak says quickly. "You mustn't come back! Don't come back!"

"This spell will end. That I promise you!" she says, and lets go of her farewells.

She hears her friend gasping for air to say something, but she doesn't look back. Armed with her gnawing rage, she runs over the dead branches that have been mangled into barricades. Her face is cut, her toes like ice, her tears frozen to her cheeks. Yet even the throbbing begins to die; the frost has numbed all pain. Days and nights have mirrored themselves, and she no longer knows where the forest ends.

The woman drags her lurching body on, still hearing the echoing sounds of Deev in the distance. She takes out the stiff red fingers from her cloak; groaning, she breathes into them.

The path that carried ice and death is now becoming more clear, and green. A cawing sound from above startles her, then another. The woman stops in her tracks. She is standing on soil leading to a vast emerald meadow. A *mirage,* she thinks.

In her delirium she laughs a laugh unfamiliar to herself, then falls to the ground, sees and feels nothing.

PART TWO

THREE DAYS AND THREE nights later, the woman finally opens her eyes and finds an old woman with light-bronze hair sitting at a nearby chair.

"Ah," the old woman says in a raspy voice, letting go of her short hair. "At last."

"Where. . . ?"

"Save your strength," says the old woman. "Some children found you by the meadow, and we brought you here, to my cottage. Rest, I'll bring you some broth."

Moments later, she returns with a bowl of steam and says, "You'll soon have some color in you."

Every mouthful of soup the other swallows is like balm to her weary body. "Thank you!" she whispers feeling only half empty.

"Where am I?"

"The Upper Lands of Nur," answers the old woman, her green cat's eyes aglow. "Eat your soup."

The younger one obeys and falls back to sleep.

THE OLD WOMAN ENTERS with a tray of tea and oatmeal the following morn. She pulls aside the drapes, flooding the room with light.

"I'm known as Hedda around here," she says as she opens the window for fresh air.

"Birds," whispers the other, and lets their chirping sounds replace the images and thunders of the Deev that invaded her dreams through the night.

"Licorice root," says Hedda, looking at the woman's frowns after she sips her tea. "It'll give you strength. Come on, sit up." Fortunately, the cinnamon oatmeal sufficiently masks the bitter tea.

By late afternoon, the woman makes her way into the rustic kitchen as Hedda is placing logs into her wood stove. "Smells delicious," she says, holding on to the doorway.

"Ah." Hedda nods. "Saves me a trip upstairs."

"How can I repay all you've done for me?" she asks Hedda, sitting down at the old wooden table.

"Already have," says the old woman with a straight face. "Was getting tired of seeing you in bed."

A couple of teacups and a plate of biscuits lie on the table. "More licorice root?" the woman asks with a grimace.

"It got you walking, didn't it?" answers Hedda, throwing her a quick glance.

The younger one unties her long black curls from behind, letting them fall heavily on her shoulders.

"Just some chamomile this time. . . . Now," says Hedda, resting her fists on her hips. "Where do you come from?"

"From the forest by the meadows."

Hedda nods. "Ah, a forest dweller," she says dryly. "And the cuts on your face and hands? Do they have an origin?"

The other's eyes darken as she sips in silence. "Do you know where I can find the Hayulah?"

"What do you want with the Hayulah?" Hedda asks, eyes narrowing.

"Do you know him?"

"What makes you think it's a *him*?" she asks after a pause, leaning back in her chair, her piercing gaze unwavering.

"A woman?"

Hedda laughs wryly. "Would you even recognize the Hayulah standing before you? . . . What is it you want?"

"She's cast a spell over the forest, covering it with black frost, guarded by the Fourth Wind of Ice. Most of the forest is dead. What's left isn't going to survive for long."

"And that's why you're here?"

The younger woman nods, then mumbles, "I was also running from the Deev."

"The Deev?" Hedda's voice is as sharp as her glare. "What does the Deev want with you?"

"My ears," the woman says, looking at Hedda but not seeing her.

"Why your ears?"

"They've heard the song of the Nightingale, who only sang at midnight."

"And?"

"Its voice still rings in my ears. The beauty of it has caused many to weep. Others became bound to the forest, and numbers turned mad with love. When word of the Midnight Nightingale spread through the trees, the Deevs told their masters, 'There is to be no other Nightingale save our own,' they said, even though their late and beloved Bird had long since perished. They ordered the capture of the Midnight Bird, along with anyone who had heard the melodies, ripping off their ears and tossing the rest of their torn bodies to the beasts."

"Well," says Hedda after a moment, eyes lost into the distance. "You're here now. Free from the Deev." Her words are as distant as her stare.

"Do you know where the Hayulah lives?" the woman asks Hedda, who locks her eyes onto her own. "Lives?" she says hoarsely, with raised eyebrows. "Or live?"

"There're more than one?"

"Are you searching for the Hayulah of the Crow? Or the Cliffs?" the old woman answers cooly, not releasing her haunting eyes. "Maybe the Hayulah of the Deep? The Lava? Or perhaps the Hayulah of the Abyss? Which one is the one you seek?"

All color drains from the younger woman's face.

"I need to fetch some tomatoes before the light leaves us completely," Hedda says, picking up a large basket from the kitchen counter.

She leaves the other in the kitchen, who, running to catch up, asks, "Which one laid the spell on the forest?" She finds Hedda among the tall tomato vines.

"Judging from the direction from which that warrior charged past these parts, my guess would be the Hayulah of the Crow," Hedda's voice rises from below as she snips three ripe tomatoes from a stem near the ground.

"Do you know where I can find this Hayulah of the Crow?"

"Yes," says Hedda, turning to her walnut tree. "At least his fort."

"Can you show me?"

"I'll take you there at daybreak." The old woman lays her basket on the ground, removes a long black pipe from her pocket and lights it, reaches for a telescope resting against the tree, and aims it at the sky. "Take a look. Go on, tell me what you see!"

The other peers through the lens. "I've never seen them so near," she says. "How long have you been following these stars?"

"Lost count," says Hedda, blowing out a stream of white smoke. "Long. Even as a little girl. They've lead me here."

"They speak to you?"

"They speak to *you* now!"

The younger woman returns to the eyepiece as Hedda sinks onto a rocking chair, releasing another thick puff of smoke. "Every night, they shimmer," she continues. "Every night, they pour their voices down to us. You'd think they'd be sick of it by now. Sick of us. Yet only a few listen. The birds listen. They look to the Silvery River to lead them.

"Stars unfolding a blindfolded past. I've spent countless nights in this very seat, imagining what lies beyond the sky we see now. Ever wonder what today's stars look like? Which ones are missing? What new formations have formed?

"And even when we find our paths drawn by a sky that *was*, that same sky cloaks the sky that *is*, somewhere beyond our reach."

With those words, the old woman retires to her abode.

The other lies in the grass and feels the night sky pulling her towards its limitless stars.

"Tell me your secrets. You know mine."

PART THREE

"THE RIVER," MUMBLES THE woman to herself. She hears its roar. Hedda is leading the way, and she follows her steps. How long has it been since she's heard the sound of flowing water, a sound that once existed in her forest? Where has their river gone?

The old woman hasn't said a word since they left her abode an hour ago. She finally breaks her silence once they reach the vast river. "I must rest here," she says and sits on a large rock.

The other drops her cloak to the ground and nears the edge of the river. She holds her hand against the current. What if she were to lie in the river and let it carry her away? Where would it take her? She lifts a handful of clear water to her face and smiles.

"Let's go now," Hedda says soon after. "It's not much further."

Their journey continues in the direction of the current.

This is where the river would have taken me? the woman asks herself when they near a great wall enclosing the water.

"This is it," Hedda tells her, though she receives only a blank stare in response. "This wall is an extension of the great fort that lies below." She leads the way again towards the perimeter of a lookout.

Where there must once have been a waterfall now stands the great white wall leading down to white marble grounds surrounding a blue-domed building.

"The Fort of the Hayulah of the Crow," says Hedda, her eyes glittering.

"Thank you," says the other when she feels her speech return to her.

"It's your life," Hedda says with an aloof shrug.

"And I owe it to you."

"Yes," the old woman says, and leaves with a hidden smile.

THE WOMAN SEARCHES THE grounds and finds a stairway that leads down to the fort grounds. Yet despite her efforts, the entryways to the fort itself remain concealed from her. Someone must know the secret, she thinks. She makes her way towards the nearby meadow-hills. The tall grass brushes against her legs, dancing to the winds. The playful breeze accompanies her. "What lies on the other side of this hill?" she asks the breeze.

"Don't you hear it?"

"What?"

"I'm carrying the echoes to you."

The woman stops and listens. "I hear you," she tells the breeze.

"Which part of me?"

"The part that sounds like a breeze."

"I bear infinite tones."

The woman closes her eyes and listens again. "I hear the soft sound of a breeze!" she says dully, and continues her way.

When she reaches the heights of the hill, her gaze falls upon a blue sea. The breeze dances about her.

"I did hear hints of these waves in you," she whispers to it.

"You listened like most do," answers the breeze, "perceiving a mere layer of what I carry. And even when you heard beyond, you didn't trust it."

The breeze sweeps by and through the tall grass.

In the distance, the woman sees another female figure sitting by a rock at the shore and rushes forward to meet her. "May I sit with you?" she asks.

"If you wish," responds the silver woman.

She climbs on to the rock and sits next to the silver woman, who is immersed waist high in water. Her silver locks float about her.

"A sea dweller?" she asks when she notices the small scales that are covering the skin of the silver woman, who offers no response.

"Do you rest here often?" asks the woman.

"Only when I need to see."

"See what?"

The sea woman points to the white bird that has been gliding above just before it whirls into a sudden dive toward its prey in the sea and makes its way back to the sky to await the next quarry over the blue water in the noonday sun. The sea woman skims her tail in and out of the water, her fin gracefully drawing the surrounding waters into a beautiful spiral. "As a little girl, I feared these birds, never knowing when or where they'd plunge into my world."

"You're blessed," says the other. "You see things below and above the waters."

"I'm one with the life below, in ways not even your dreams can imagine," the sea woman says. "Yet I can't see the world below until I sit on this rock—to hear my thoughts and see my blindness."

"As a child I've heard many tales about the enchanting voices of the sea dwellers," says the other after a time.

"We no longer bear such voices."

"No one?"

"Our voices came from the pearls we once possessed in our throats. Once they were taken, all song was lost. There are no pearls to be found, not even in the throats of those born thereafter."

"Who would do this?"

"The people of the Crow. Our songs carried many of their men to safe shores—men who were lost at sea as death lingered. Yet somewhere in the flow of time, we began losing our families. Word spread through the sea dwellers that our kin had been, not lost, but taken. The hidden mystery of our voices had been discovered. Soon the sea became a bearer of great ships. One by one, pearls were ripped from our throats. None were spared, not even our children. When they had all they wanted, we were hurled into the waters, our blood becoming one with the big deep. But they hadn't foreseen the void, the absence of our songs. Some attempted to replace the pearls, but no matter how they forced them into our throats, they wouldn't stay in place. And so we remain, without pearl, empty of song—only our lost destiny, living memories of memories."

A breeze brushes them by, and the sea woman turns to it. "You're searching for someone," she says.

"I'm looking for Rostam," says the other, raising her head. "Have you seen the warrior on a steed?"

"No, but the rains have."

"When?"

"The night before last. They washed his blood into the sea."

"I must find him."

"You seek his corpse?"

"He's not dead."

"The wind spoke otherwise."

"What wind?"

"The Wind of Night. Speaking of the battle with the Hayulah of the Crow. How the warrior nearly vanquished him. But as always, the Hayulahs never work alone. And their joint powers are no match for anyone, not even the warrior Rostam."

"He can't be."

"I must leave," the sea woman says, and slides into the sea.

"Wait," says the other. "Do you know how to enter the Fort?"

"If you're looking for him, he's not there. He's with the Hayu-lah of the Deep."

"Where can I find him?"

"In the Deep."

"Below?"

The sea woman nods. "In the Lands of Ice."

"How can I get there?"

"Wait here," says the sea woman and disappears into the waters.

At dusk, the sea woman returns with a dolphin by her side. "Kayahn will take you," she says, and bids farewell, but not before handing her a strand of seaweed. "Eat this underwater, and you'll find air beneath and cover from the cold."

"Thank you—"

But the sea woman is already gone.

"There's just enough seaweed for you to survive the trip," Kayahn tells the woman. "Once you eat it, we'll have to hurry."

She nods and submerges herself. Salty water gushes into her mouth as she takes a bite of the seaweed. Too distracted by the sickening tastes she is swallowing, she at first doesn't notice she is breathing under water.

"We go now," says Kayahn. "Hold on to my back with one hand."

For days they have been speeding through the down under, slowly moving into frigid temperatures, when a shadow suddenly passes by them, and a heavy blow slams into her side, breaking her hold on Kayahn. The enormous frame, wildly moving about, sends her into a whirlwind of bubbles. Another body, a seal, brushes against her. The woman breaks free from the agitated water and swims towards the light. She pulls herself unto a block of ice floating above. Holding her shaking body, she searches for Kayahn, who finally emerges.

"We must hurry," says Kayahn.

"What *was* that?"

"Cynric," says Kayahn. "But he hunts another now. We must go before he returns!"

Just as she reenters the water, her eyes fall upon a magnificent iceberg in the distance, rising high in the vast blue of the sky.

"The Fortress of the Hayulah of the Deep," says Kayahn, following her gaze.

"He lives on an iceberg?"

"Within," he says. "Quick, we must reach it before the seaweed runs its course."

As they move close to the Great Fortress, they descend deeper along shimmering ice walls that seem to stretch down with no end. At last they swim into an opening in the curved folds and pass through a canal that leads them to an ice cave. They peek out of the water and breathe the icy air. The woman lifts herself onto the ice ground.

"Don't forget what I told you," Kayahn says.

"I won't forget," she says. "Or what you've done for me."

The dolphin sinks back into the water.

PART FOUR

THE SEAWEED ISN'T PROTECTING her from the bitter cold anymore. The dark passageway out of the cave leads to a haze of glimmers in the distance. By the time she reaches the glows, her body is shivering uncontrollably. She stretches her shaky hand through the beams and feels the heat, then immerses her entire body in their warming embrace.

Even when she's fully dry, she finds it difficult to let go of the scintillating glows. Yet the Hayulah of the Deep is somewhere beyond the lights; thus, she must carry onwards.

A melodious female voice fills the air. She follows it to where the haze turns blue, then clear.

Before her stretches an orchard.

"In an iceberg?" she murmurs to herself.

The voice belongs to the Blue Mahoe tree, adorned with orange-red flowers that move in the light breeze. A path of rounded, flat auburn pebbles marks the way through a maze of trees. She picks up one of the smooth and shiny pebbles. "Copper?" she says and lets it fall to the ground. The rich greens and bright flowers are even more striking against a clear blue sky containing scattered puffy clouds that emanate light.

Suddenly, from behind a date tree, she sees a profile of raised plumes.

She recalls Kayahn's warnings—*Don't look into the eyes of the peacocks*—and averts her eyes. *And no matter what, do not drink the water.*

She hurries forward. By the time she reaches the acacia tree, she can't go further. A gold-neck peacock is poised in the middle of her path, its blue train stretched high. She avoids the bird's glare but can't help glancing at its flaunting feathers that change from shades of turquoise to midnight blue. She breaks her stare and brushes by the peacock towards the mango tree.

"Do you know the way to the Hayulah of the Deep?"

"Yes," says the mango, but doesn't continue.

"Can you tell me?"

"Yes."

"*Will* you tell me?" she finally says.

"Within the Garden Palace," says the mango. "Past the baobabs."

The copper pebbles lead her out of the Orchard Maze towards a walkway enclosed by two canals. The soothing sound of the clear, streaming water flirts with the thirst she's been withstanding since the salty waters of the Deep.

The walkway leads to a waterfall she must traverse if she is to enter the Garden Palace, but she would first have to make her way past the two peacocks that are striding before the waters.

The first, arrayed in silver and green, wears a silver crest embedded with small diamonds. It turns its fiery orange neck towards the woman and doesn't let go of her gaze. Yet it's the second peacock whose deep mauves and blues captivate her most. The magnificent creatures begin a slow, graceful approach, each extending velvet plumage far and wide. Tears flow from her eyes. She fights her longing to give into their fixed gaze, yet it's the peacocks who hold the power now. She smiles, bows, and turns back toward the Orchard Maze, but not before washing her face with the canal waters, allowing their fresh taste to quench her body.

How did she not see the mangoes on the ground before? She removes a small dagger from her boot and peels the skins. The sweet juices make her laugh. She leans against the magnolia, covering herself with walnuts, figs, dates, and mulberries that have fallen on the green grass. She feasts, laughs, and falls asleep.

The crickets at last announce that night has fallen. Stretched on the grass, she opens her eyes, rests her head in her palms, and begins to hum under the star-filled sky.

"Dear one," calls Anar, the pomegranate tree. She hears the words but continues her song.

"Dear one," the pomegranate calls again. This time the words enter and, like a dagger, pierce her chest. Only one other calls her "dear one"—only the oak.

"How. . . ?" she asks as she lifts herself from the ground, slowly moving towards the tree. "How do you know—"

"Who calls you 'dear one'? Cradles you to sleep? Brushes your curls? Hides you within its trunk?"

Sounds and images from the Deev, her forest, the oak, rush towards her.

"Who are you?"

"Anar."

"How do you know all this?"

"Because you've forgotten."

The woman weeps.

"Your tears may not save your friend or your land," the tree assures her, "but they do help to wash away the spell of the peacocks."

"How do you know all this? About my friend?"

"I don't know."

"Can you see the oak? Do you speak to each other?"

"No. But I carry some of the memories."

"Thank you for breaking the spell," the woman says after a moment and sits against the tree. She lifts a walnut from the ground but doesn't crack it open. "How did you grow here?"

"I don't know. My past lies hidden somewhere amid my dreams."

"How can there be this orchard in the center of an iceberg?"

"A mystery," responds Anar. "At any given moment, a new tree, as unusual and exquisite as the next, may become part of our orchard. The stones you walked on are our latest addition."

"Do you know how I can get to the Hayulah?"

"No."

"No?" says the woman, her face clouding. "Why call me out of the spell then?"

"Would you rather be *under* the spell? Oblivious?"

"Than sit here knowing I have no way of reaching the Hayulah? Forever revisiting the oak's struggle for breath amid the Deev's echoes?" the woman darkly retorts, and tosses the walnut away. "At least I was lost in the taste of these fruits."

The moon shines
with its gentle touch.
It smiles and tells her,
Dance my love, dance!
And she obeys.
And she's not alone.

PART FIVE

The woman sits by the tree whose sour cherries she has just picked. They taste of home. She smiles and has started to climb the tree again to pick more of the red delights when a rush of wind passes through the leaves and, with it, jolting, distant cries. She sees a figure in red running through the trees, spreading his screams—a tall, hairless man in loose crimson clothing who stops in his tracks near her tree. He drops to the ground, his cheek against the green grass, and stares ahead.

"You think I don't see you?" he says, not moving a muscle.

The woman falls to her hands and feet, keeping one hand close to the dagger in her boot. "Are you hurt?" she asks tentatively.

The tall man bursts into laughter that is both lengthy and tearful as he rolls about in the grass.

"Who would have thought it possible—a harmed *djinni*."

"*Djinni?*"

The *djinni* is no longer laughing. His eyes glaze over as he looks off into the sky.

"Why were you running?" she asks, drawing the hand away from her boot.

"Searching for my previous master."

"How did you lose your master?" she asks, and takes a step towards him.

"She freed me from my lamp and disappeared," the *djinni* says lifelessly, tears falling down his face.

"Why are you looking for her?"

"Only she can return me to my lamp."

"But you're *free*."

The *djinni* sobs and laughs. "Since my freedom, I've walked the grounds, filling my days, turning beggars into kings and back to beggars, giving children to the barren and robbing them later from their mothers. I reunite lost lovers, then break their bonds with one glance—all randomly chosen, on a moment's whim."

"Why?"

"I'm a *djinni*," he says and chuckles.

"But why return to your lamp?"

"Because all I want to do here is *die*," he says and begins to weep.

"Maybe you can help me," she says after watching the walnut tree soak up the *djinni*'s tears.

"Riches?"

"No," she says, and whispers, "I need to destroy the Hayulah of the Deep."

The *djinni* briefly studies her. "Not even I can destroy him," he says. "But I know one who can help you."

"Who?"

"Simurgh, the phoenix."

"How can I find her?"

"With her feather," he explains. "I can give you the feather, but I'll need something from you."

"Anything."

"One of your eyes."

"My *eye*?" she gasps, her face clouding.

"You said anything."

THE HOWLING DJINNI RUNS between the trees, leaving the woman sitting by a bonfire with an eye patch, holding a long golden feather between her fingers. She throws the feather into the flames, releasing a massive bolt of light. When it dims, she sees a large phoenix. Taller than the trees, she has the head of a dog and lion claws. Her long blue-and-gold tail dances about her in a soft rhythm.

"Why have you summoned me?" Simurgh asks, golden eyes stretched beneath a frowning brow.

"I need your help," the woman says quickly. "The forest needs your help."

"What is it you seek?"

"To kill the Hayulah of the Deep."

"You call me here to *kill*?" Simurgh exclaims with fire in her voice.

"He slew your grandson, Rostam!"

"I know," the phoenix murmurs, and turns away.

"Please. Help me destroy him."

"Why do you choose to turn to ice?" asks Simurgh. "To breath in his frozen crystals?"

"I'm not frozen, but on fire," the woman says firmly. "He must be stopped!"

"Killing him will not bring back my Rostam," says Simurgh, eyes brimming with tears. "Or your forest."

"I *beg* you!" the woman cries, dropping to her knees. "Help me."

The Simurgh paces to the trees and looks above them, her tail feathers twirling around her. She doesn't speak, she doesn't move, and neither does the woman.

"I will offer the same counsel as I once did to my grandson, who was equally as stubborn as you," the Simurgh says finally. "Three times have I witnessed the creation and destruction of this world. What you seek will not come to you by killing the Hayul-lah."

"And what *would* you have me do?" The woman's voice has risen. "How many will continue to suffer and perish? When is enough enough? I only ask you to show me how to put an end to this spell. . .please."

The Simurgh turns her fierce yellow eyes on the woman and speaks. "Then build a two-pronged arrowhead made of tamarisk. You will then face the Hayulah of the Deep and plead with him, from the purest corners of your soul, to lift his spells and release what's left of the forest. Take heed!" The voice has grown round and reverberates. "It is with earnest humility that you must present your supplications. Only kind and gentle words. Should he reject them and belittle your sincerity, then shoot your arrow directly at his eyes."

"What if I miss?"

"If your rage be born of justice, the arrow will faithfully strike its intended mark. But remember," the Simurgh adds, "it is only to be used after showing honest benevolence and a desire for peace, nothing less."

The woman nods and climbs onto the back of Simurgh, who rises into the sky with a great sweep of her wide wings and flies off to a distant lake where they find a branch of tamarisk and the woman follows the phoenix's directions for making the two-pronged arrow.

"And what of the peacocks?" the woman asks. "I can't get past them."

"Close your eye, and see through the one that is missing."

"Thank you," the woman says.

"Only a fool thanks where nothing merits it," says Simurgh, flaps her heavy wings again, and soars into the sky.

PART SIX

THE WOMAN SHUTS HER eye and turns towards the peacocks. All is dark. Where shall she step? For hours she contemplates her next move but then, little by little, begins to make out shapes and forms with her missing eye.

She passes the extravagant birds and runs through the waterfall, covering her mouth with her sleeve. Not a drop touches her lips.

"Stop!" cries a man from behind.

She turns to the voice and sees him, pale, broad-shouldered, clothed in navy blue colors and wearing a stony face.

"I wish no harm," she declares. "I wish only to speak to the Hayulah of the Deep."

The man leads her through a long corridor walled in glass behind which colorful sea creatures are darting amid brightly lit corals. They reach a large door that opens to a vast courtyard filled with fountains of milky water lilies and rows of ivory rose bushes. Beyond a knoll of white tulips, a path bordered in calla lilies lines the approach to the platinum Garden Palace.

Four women with expressionless eyes are standing guard at the palace entrance. The pale man leads the way past them into an entrance hall made entirely of glass, revealing more tropical ocean life. They fall into step behind. A spotted stingray glides gracefully beneath the woman's feet among the multitudes of fish and sea horses that surround the chamber.

An idle cheetah is sprawled out on an ornate couch in the center of the room. It raises its head, peers at the woman, and begins to lick its lithe paws.

"Whom do we have here?" asks a young voice from above.

The woman looks up and sees a boy, no older than twelve, hanging from a pole suspended from the glass ceiling.

"A woman from the forest," says one of the female guards, who have accompanied her and the man.

The woman's eye darts towards the guard, making the boy laugh.

"You don't think you just *flowed* here, do you?"

"Since you know who I am, will you afford me the same pleasure?"

"All the way here, and you don't know who I am? I thought this was going to be fun," he says in a dull tone. "Let's get it over with then."

He hurls his body into another loop over the pole and flashes to the ground, throws his arms out wide, and exclaims, "Presenting the Hayulah of the Deep."

"You?" the woman gasps, gaping at him.

"Oh! I guess you're amusing after all!" he says smiling, and leaps towards a seat of golden velvet. "Now—what do you want?"

"I come to you because our forest is in pain."

"Yes, that forest *was* a pain."

The woman pauses a moment before she says, "I'm begging for your compassion. Please lift the spell from the forest."

"But it's such a *good* spell. The old crow and I worked really hard on that one. . . . Oh, and you've just missed him, too. He left with his wife, the Hayulah of the Abyss. Her spells are almost as good as mine. Hm. Too bad they're gone. They would've been quite 'tickled' by your little visit, as Lady Abyss would say."

"We're *dying!*"

"You bore me," says the Hayulah, looking up at a sea turtle.

The woman's eye darkens. With lightning speed, she tears the bow from her cloak and aims an arrow at him.

He roars a wicked laugh. Neither he, the cheetah, nor the guards seem alarmed.

"Oh, good! You really are entertaining," he says with a bright face, then hotly whispers, "Kill me—kill you." He raises his palm up to the glass. The translucent ceiling clouds over to show moving images of the woman eating sour cherries in the orchard. Next, she sees a little girl, with wet blonde curls, running through gushing fountains, squealing in excitement. "Kill me—kill her," the Hayu-

lah continues. He is on his back, facing the screen, which now re-
veals several children jumping, splashing, and laughing in the free-
flowing water. ". . .Kill *them*, too!"

The woman lowers her aim slowly and leaves. The guffaws of
the Hayulah follow her back to the Orchard Maze, back to the
mango tree.

"*You* don't belong here," the woman says, shouting at the trees.
"What's happened to you? Wake up!"

She moves from one tree to another, touching their bark, shaking their branches.

The date tree leans down and slaps her body, throwing her
against the palm. "It's *you* who doesn't belong here."

She lifts her aching back from the ground and limps towards
the haze, away from the orchard, back to the warm light and to the
ice cave.

She screams a deafening cry and falls to the icy ground.

"Come," says a voice from the waters.

"Kayahn," the woman whispers in shivers.

PART SEVEN

KAYAHN RACES THROUGH THE water with the woman lying face down on his back. She can still taste the seaweed he brought for her to make the journey. His skin feels warm against her cheeks. She caresses him tenderly, kisses him on his back, and falls asleep. Days pass before they reach land.

"The shores here are calm," he says as they near a large rock outcrop in the water. "I hope you find your way."

She holds the dolphin in her arms, and they embrace. Their farewells linger, but at last she watches his glistening body disappear into the shimmering sea. She lies on the rocks and looks on after him until she can no longer see his fins in the distance. Waves wash over her, rocking her long hair back and forth. And so she remains for hours.

In time, she sits up, slips the dagger from her boot, and cuts off all her hair. The loose strands drift over the water, and she watches them on the waves until a sea turtle's head appears from below, devours them, and vanishes.

She leaves the rocks and heads inland through a pasture, the sea behind her, the mountains ahead, and weeps.

"Tell me about the sea," says a voice from her wet hand.

"Why don't you look for yourself?" she answers stiffly.

"I can't."

"I can dip you in the water," she says at last.

"Then I'll no longer be a teardrop."

"You'd be the sea."

"But I'd be dead. And you just gave me life."

"How long will you survive on my hand?"

"As long as I can."

"It won't be long like this," she says as she lets the teardrop fall onto the leaf of a nearby bush.

"Are you going home?"

"No."

"Where is your home?"

"Nowhere," says the woman, "and everywhere."

"Where're you going, then?"

"I'm searching for Simurgh."

"Where?"

"I don't know."

"Why are you searching for her?"

"I want her to eat me."

"Are you insane?"

The woman says nothing.

"How little you value your gift," says the teardrop bitterly. "I'd give anything to be free as you are."

"What makes you think I'm free?"

"Why, you. . .you can run on the ground for as far as you wish. You can swim in the sea and tell of its tales. You're not bound to this leaf."

"A leaf that keeps you a teardrop," she points out.

". . .How can you dismiss your freedom so easily?"

"I'm not. I wasn't always free to walk the land without death at my feet. But is freedom really of one kind?" says the woman, staring off into space. "I may be free from the Deev, here and now, but I'm not free. Not when my friend isn't, nor the forest, lands, or seas. And though I'd cherish freedom from the spells, would we really be free even then?"

"So you'd rather seek death."

"Not death, freedom."

"And you think you'll find freedom in the stomach of a phoenix?"

"No. But my search will begin there. If I can be one with Simurgh and see what she's seen through the ages, I may understand what she was trying to tell me. And then my search will begin."

"What kind of search?"

"The search for freedom of spirit."

". . .Tell me more."

Author's Note:

Persian legends have been infused into this tale, most of which are derived from the work of Ferdowsi's *Shahnameh*—a collection of poems about Persian history and mythology, starting from the beginning of time through the Islamic conquest of Persia in the seventh century.

Glossary

Agha: Commonly used after a man's name—equivalent to "Mr."

Albaloo khoshkeh: Dried sour cherries.

Amreh Jensi: Sexual cause.

Azizam: Term of endearment, means 'my dear'.

Báb: The founder of the Bábi Faith and the forerunner of Bahá'u'lláh, the founder of the Bahá'í Faith.

Bahá'u'lláh: The founder of the Bahá'í Faith.

Bahh-bahh! Roya janeh gol!: Bahh-bahh is an expression of delight. The remainder of the sentence can be translated: "Roya dear, who is like a flower!"

Baluch: From Baluchistan, a large, mountainous, and arid region covering southeast Iran, southwest Afghanistan, and southwest Pakistan. The Baluch people have for the most part maintained their cultural identity and independence. Their attire is similar to the Shalvar Khamis worn in Pakistan.

Chador: Veil.

Chaee: Persian black tea.

Chaee Khaneh: Tea house.

Chaghaleh badoom: Unripe almonds.

Dai jan: "Dear uncle."

Dizin: A ski resort in the Alborz mountain range, two hours north of Tehran.

Doogh: A fizzy yoghurt drink.

Estop rangui: Game of tag. The tagger calls a color, and all run to find and touch the color before they're tagged.

Farsi: The Iranian language.

Ghand: Sugar cubes.

Gojeh sabz: Green sour plums.

Googoosh: A famous Iranian pop singer.

Haj Agha: A title given to men who have made their pilgrimage to Mecca.

Ich bin in Wien geboren: German for "I was born in Vienna."

Jan or *joon*: A term of endearment that usually follows a person's name. Both mean "dear."

Joob: Water channels that run on the sides of most streets in Tehran, carrying rain water and melted snow from the surrounding mountains.

Kamar Shol: A term for impotence.

Kesh-bazi: Chinese jump rope.

Khaleh: Usually, a mother's sister, but also used when referring to a close family friend.

Khanum: Commonly used after a woman's name, equivalent to "Ms."

Khoda: God.

Lavashak: Natural fruit roll-ups.

Lay-lay: Hopscotch.

Limu shirin: Literally, "sweet lemons," which look like small grapefruits and have a bittersweet taste.

Mensch: a German expression similar to "man."

Mirch nahin, kali mirch nahin: "No chili, no black pepper" in Urdu.

Nadjes: Applied to anything considered "unclean" under Islamic law (ex: dogs, pork, Bahá'ís).

Nanneh: Village term for "Ma" that is also applied to housekeepers, who were usually from the villages.

Nisiri'd-Din Shah Qajar: Shah of Persia, who reigned between 1848 and 1896.

Noon barbari: Iranian flatbread.

Panir Irani: Iranian feta cheese—similar to Bulgarian feta.

Pasdaran: The Islamic Revolutionary Guards.

Peerashkis: Pirogues.

Poffak Namaki: Cheese Doodles.

Strassenbahn: German for "light rail."

Shomal: Up north, by the shores of the Caspian Sea.

Tahchin: A Persian dish consisting of yellow rice with yoghurt-based chicken.

Takhteh: Backgammon.

Tambreh hendi: Pure tamarind.

Tanab-bazi: Jump rope.

Toll: A German expression similar to "great."

Vielen Dank: German for "Many thanks."

Ya, Ich verstehe: German for "Yes, I understand."

Ya Khoda: Oh, God.

Zahedan: A southeastern city in Iran and the capital of Sistan and Baluchistan province, located near the borders of Pakistan and Afghanistan.

ABOUT THE AUTHOR

Roya Movafegh is a multi-media artist. Her work explores the dynamics of assimilation as well as the multiple facets of cultural identity. In addition to her photo publication in Eileen William's *Wishes in Black & White* featured on *Oprah*, her work has also appeared in *Them=Us: Photographic Journeys Across Our Cultural Boundaries*. Born in Austria to Iranian parents, she and her family moved to Tehran in 1976 only to escape it five years later due to the persecutions they faced as Bahá'ís. From an early age, she learned what it meant to be a foreigner, a person on the run, a refugee, and an immigrant. After living in Germany, the United States, and Canada, she moved to Harlem, New York, in 1998, where she founded The Young Harlem Photographers, a photography workshop for children and youth, which won the *New York Times* award at the Art of Change Group Show.

Co-founder with Mehr Mansuri of The Children's Theatre Company of New York (CTC) (www.childrenstheatrecompany.org), CTC has been featured on *Good Morning America*, CNN, and the *NY1*

Parenting Report, and has performed several concerts for UNICEF with Nelson Mandela, James Earl Jones, Harry Belafonte, Wynton Marsalis, and other world dignitaries. They have also made appearances on NBC's *Today Show, Sesame Street*, and *Reading Rainbow*.

She has also developed several art-based programs for children and youth dedicated to endeavors that highlight their inherent nobility, raise social awareness, and encourage becoming agents of change in the world they are inheriting.

Her thirty-nine-year journey has finally culminated in her debut novel, *The People With No Camel*, in which she not only gives voice to the plight of the Bahá'í community in Iran, but addresses concepts of freedom in the West.

To Learn More

To learn about the latest developments of *The People With No Camel* visit *www.thepeoplewithnocamel.com*

Other works by Roya Movafegh:
www.royamovafegh.com

For further information about the situation of the Bahá'ís of Iran, visit the following:
http://question.bahai.org
http://denial.bahai.org

ACKNOWLEDGMENTS

These words of thanks only touch the surface of the level of gratitude I feel towards the individuals mentioned here, some of whose names have been changed to protect them and their families.

My deepest thanks to my parents, whose mere mention brings me to tears. For the purpose of this book you swallowed your own pain, time and time again, to answer my many calls to revisit painful memories—some so safely tucked away that they have been forgotten, others as fresh as open wounds. Thank you for walking side by side with me during this endeavor with heart and soul. I thank my father for giving me wings to soar into the vast sky, who still to this day sees anything I create as a masterpiece. I thank my mother for giving me practical feet when I need to land, who so patiently and lovingly went through the chapters of this book to assist with the details. I give thanks to my brother Joubin, my friend and childhood partner in surviving, and navigating through, a messy world. Thank you! Thank God for your humor! Thank God you are my brother!

To my soulmate Hooshmand, my confidant, my heart: This book would not have been written without your unwavering, loving support. Your insight and passion are a constant inspiration. So grateful to be treading more journeys with you and our children. To our precious daughters, Lia and Ariane, for your patience during some of the hours that should have been yours. I will not forget your loving hugs, your understanding nods. I'll always remember your loving kisses, my dear Ariane, during my hours of writing. And your caring voice, my dear Lia: "OK, Mommy, we'll close the door, so you can write your story." Who knew that my eight-year-old would become my most devoted supporter and publicist?

A profound sense of gratitude to the courageous and persevering souls: Omid, Iran, Sahar, Sarajollah H., and their families, who allowed me to share their stories. To Rashid Mostaghim and Mahdokht Ghazanfari, who recounted the plight of the Iranian Bahá'í community with detail, photographs, and song. Mr. Mostaghim, I will always remember your fervent chant of Deegar Che Ghami which brought us all to tears. May the world hear all your voices, your sacrifices, your passions, your hearts, your love for something you hold greater than yourselves. . . .

I owe a debt of gratitude to Hamid and Nasser, who risked everything to help us and others escape. Without you, this book would not have been written—the stories not shared. Thank you!

To my four grandparents, whose love and influences are coiled within my fabric, to my grandmother Pari joon for being the pillar of strength that you are, thank you for your continuous prayers and your nurturing presence. To my aunt Sheida for inspiring and assisting me in my excursion through the Shahnameh and your consistent encouragement. Thank you to my aunt Soheila and my cousins Siba Shakib, Schabi Girard, and Sandra Schmeil for their loving assistance and support.

Immeasurable thanks to Cris Beam, who saw, felt, and believed in the story—and who so artfully helped me tap into places I would have rather not traversed at the time. I can never thank you enough for traveling through this journey with me. Grateful to have had you as my guide, as my editor, as my friend. Thank you to the literary agent for shredding my first three paragraphs to pieces at a writer's workshop. Without that painful experience, I would not have been lead to Cris. My heartfelt thanks to my friend Azadeh A., who picked up my droopy spirit after the aforementioned workshop. Thank you for your staunch support of this book and for introducing me to Cris! And a note of gratitude to Meira Pentermann for reaching out to me the way you did to express your support. And a great big thank-you to Leora Solkin-Smith. You encouraged me to stay true to my gut and not compromise my work to fit the mainstream.

My warmest gratitude to Barry Sheinkopf at Full Court Press for his meticulous editing and book design. Your professionalism has been invaluable. Your guidance, especially in the form of storytelling, has been a gift, a delight, and full of insight. Thank you!

Thank you, Diane Ala'i, for your time and attention. To Taraneh Ashraf for so lovingly assisting me during my research. Thank you both for everything you do to bring about awareness to the plight of the Bahá'ís in Iran! Thank you to Michael Penn, whose warmth and consistent encouragement made all the difference.

A wholehearted thank-you to my classmates in Iran, who didn't forget me. . .to dear Ghazal, who found me after twenty-seven years (thank you, Google!) and brought back so much of what I thought I'd lost. . .to Parvaneh, who remembered every detail. . .to Ariane who never held a grudge after our last conversation as ten-year-olds. . .to Julia, Britta, Susan, Sheila, Mariam, and Leyli for writing back. Grateful for your love, your friendship, and for filling a part of me that had remained empty for almost thirty years.

To my first and oldest friend, Max Jezo-Parovsky: I choke up when I think of your generous spirit and deep friendship. I'm incredibly grateful for your time, your stunning design of the book cover, and your masterful trailer of *The People With No Camel*. I cannot properly express how much your help, your brilliant artistry, and humor mean to me. And thank you to your father for bringing us together after googling my last name from that little piece of paper he found—after twenty-four years.

What would I do without you, Talia Johnson! Like an angel by my side, you have carried me through the virtual world with patience and grace. Thank you for all your hard work on the website, for expanding my horizons on so many levels, for your guidance, and above all, for your wholehearted dedication to see this book reach hearts, for being there every time I called for help, and for your friendship.

A very special thanks to the powerful music of Zoe Keating, Moby, TaliaSafa, Luke Slott, Eva Maria Rauter, and M. Ward, whom I listened to on repeat while writing. Thank you for inspiring the words to flow onto the pages, especially during the times the well felt dry. The chapters will forever have your music interwoven with the words. Special thanks to Zoe Keating for allowing me to use her enchanting track "Legions (Aftermath)" for the trailer. You are truly gracious!

Immensely grateful to Mehr Mansuri, thank you for your presence, love, fervor, and staunch friendship. I will never forget the day you read my work to me—when I could no longer see the words. Thank you for sharing your powerful voice for the trailer and audiobook. I have learned so much from you. You are truly a beautiful treasure! And thank you for always having my back.

To my dearest Kristina Golmohammadi, thank you for creating a dramatic reading of this book and for bringing it to life in a whole new way. Your strength, passion, and extraordinary spirit are a continued source of energy for me.

My expression of thanks to Muni Tahzib for her consistent offers of assistance, which ultimately led me to Barry Sheinkopf.

Deeply touched by Shohreh Aghdashloo, Neda Armian, and Shidan Majidi for their time and their moving reviews of *The People With No Camel*.

Thank you to Steve Francis at Stush Music for your valuable assistance in the voiceover recordings.

To my publicist and friend Melisa Tropeano LaTour, at MTL Communications, thank you for your passion, fearless spirit, and vitality.

To my beloved friends, too numerous to mention by name, I am truly blessed to have you all in my life! So grateful for your play date offers so that I could write; your willingness to knock on any door in case someone answered; whether you are far or near, your love, encouragement, and enthusiasm have fueled me countless times! Included in this long list are: Azita Shahidi—your heart, assistance, and selflessness are awe-inspiring. You are an angel! Behrooz Shahidi, your friendship and support have meant so much! And thank you for the photograph you took for this book. Nazish Ahmed, many thanks for answering my random calls to revive forgotten details of Pakistan. Zutta Codjoe, like family you assisted me in my juggle of motherhood and writing. Thank you Lyn Dexheimer for your time and for being my extra pair of eyes. Thanks to Keyvan Mahjoor, Julie Hartigan, Vrinda Deva, Christie Ryan, Lori Tharps, Kate Digby, Bruce Grover, Daniel Stee, and Michea Caye—I'm grateful for your loving support! And finally, Bahiyyih Lawson, who is the reason I started to write. To my friends and practitioners Terryann Nikides, Leigh Muro, Susan Gala, and Karen Atkins, who have lovingly assisted me through my long journey of healing. Your love made so much possible! To Becky Murphy, you always found a way to let me know that you were there—and even now after your passing, you still let me know. . .I love you deeply, Becky.

To my teachers Monique Régimbald-Zeiber, Tim Clark, and Peter Rist, who not only opened up the vast world of the arts for me but accompanied me in finding my own forms of expression. You were there for me in a way that you may never realize. You gave me voice, a voice I thought had been strangled by my experiences in and out of Iran. Your guidance and incessant support allowed me to channel my pain and anger into a voice that wasn't going to remain unheard. I'm honored to have had you all as my teachers and will forever be grateful.

And finally, to the great poetess Tahirih, my heroine, whose courage and fierce strength I drew upon when the writing became the hardest.

This book has been set in Hoefler's *Requiem*,

derived from a set of inscriptional capitals

appearing in Ludovico Vicentino degli Arrighi's

1523 writing manual, *Il Modo de Temparere le Penne.*